mistletoe
mail

Cover illustrations by Teodora Dimitrova

Cover design by Ali Salvino

Editing by Happily Editing Anns

CONTENTS

AUTHOR'S NOTE

This book contains subject matter that some people may find triggering. A list of the main potential triggers can be found on Katherine's website:

http://www.katherinejayauthor.com

Please note, triggers are not listed here to avoid spoilers for the book.

PLAYLIST

Merry Christmas - Ed Sheeran, Elton John
Underneath The Tree - Kelly Clarkson
Have Yourself a Merry Little Christmas - Michael Bublé
If You Love Her - Forest Blakk
Jingle Bell Rock - Bobby Helms
Wildcard - Miley Cyrus
Unstoppable - Sia
Little Do You Know - Alex & Sierra
My December - Lincoln Park
ON MY MIND - ALEX WARREN, ROSÉ
Rewrite The Stars - James Arthur, Anne Marie
Wings - Birdy
Waves - Dean Lewis
Sweet Child O' Mine - Guns N' Roses

To all the non believers (in true love),
sometimes all you need is an Australian
in a Santa coat handing out toys... and
maybe a little Mistletoe.

IMPORTANT NOTE

Mistletoe Mail takes place in Australia and the USA with an Australian male main character (MMC) and an American female main character (FMC). Because of this, chapters in the MMC's POV have been written in Australian English and the chapters in the FMC's POV have been written in American English.

PROLOGUE
Jenna

AGE 19

The techno beat softens as I traipse through the opulent mansion, escaping the chaos for a moment of peace. Pushing deeper inside, I'm surprised to find that it's empty. There are hundreds of people outside.

Did I miss a "do not enter" sign?

I shiver at the silence. I've never actually been here, but this hockey house is known for throwing epic parties, and I've heard a lot about the inside of their palace-like home. It's not usually off-limits. Though considering today is the Fourth of July foam pit party, the rules may have changed.

I wouldn't want anyone trudging through my house in bubble-soaked attire. But who would have guessed the guys on the hockey team were forward thinkers like that?

My gaze rakes over the luxurious furnishings—the marble mantel, the grand mahogany dining table—and my mouth twitches in amusement. *What in the interior design loving hell?*

Did I stumble into the twilight zone?

When I finally reach the living room, my jaw drops at the eight-seater sectional sofa and accompanying massage chairs, but I shouldn't be surprised. Grateful is a better reaction. I'm practically drooling at the comfort staring back at me. With a moan, I take a step closer just as an external door opens and the thumping beat of an unfamiliar remix filters inside.

"Jenna! Are you in there? I want you to meet someone," my roommate, Penelope, calls from the threshold, and I wince, my longing stare locked on the plush couch, begging to be sat on. I *was* so *close*.

If ignoring her was an option, I'd continue on my way, but Pen on a sober day is pushy. Pen drunk...I have no hope in hell of avoiding this.

Glancing over my shoulder, I pray for someone to distract her, but when she calls out again, excitement clear in her voice, I relent.

"Jenna!"

"Yeah. I'm here, and I'm coming."

"That's what she said." Pen's roaring laughter soars over the music, and I'd join in if she wasn't dead wrong.

She didn't say that at all. *She* being *me*. Because tonight has been a shit show to say the least, and I'm done. If I wasn't waiting for Penelope's boyfriend to drive us home, I'd be long gone. I'm not feeling it tonight. Nothing is going to pull me from this funk.

Adjusting my boobs in my tight black romper, I blow out a breath and make my way toward the yard, knowing what's coming. Pen's trying to set me up. *Again.* She feels bad after her cousin told the world—or at least, the sophomore theater cohort—that I was bad in bed. All because he wanted more and I wasn't interested. It didn't help that I may have mentioned his best friend was a more alluring option.

It's my fault. I get it. I bruised his ego. But the truth is...I don't care about the rumors he's spreading. I'm a good fuck. The annoying thing is that now, I don't know if people want me for me, or to test out Brant's theory.

I've come to the realization that I might have to wait until the gossip dies down before hooking up again. And the idea of that sucks.

"Hurry up," Pen calls out as I'm turning the corner, her annoyance morphing into a grin.

"It's not my fault this place is huge—I was at the other end of the house."

"You're here now and this is Jack." Pen grabs the guy beside her, thrusting him toward me as she bounces on her toes. "Say hi, Jack."

Jack's eyes widen and I force a smile, leaning back. Pen pushed him so hard that if he wasn't a giant of a man, we'd be face-to-face. Instead, my eyes lock on the tee pulled tight over his muscular chest before lifting to his face. And *hello, gorgeous.*

"Hey. Jenna, was it?" He smiles and I do a double take. His deep voice has a twang to it that I wasn't expecting.

"That's me." I wave, tilting my head in intrigue. "What is that accent?"

"I'm Aussie."

"You're Australian?" I gape, a giddiness running through me.

"Sure am."

"What are you doing *here*?"

Pen waves at me from behind Jack's shoulder and I roll my eyes. "Excuse me a second, Jack. Yes, you're free to leave, Pen. I'm a big girl."

"Thank you. Have a good night, Jack."

Jack spins to watch Penelope walk away, and when she's gone, he turns back to face me, his expression wary. "She's not subtle at all."

"No, she's not. And full transparency, you're the fourth guy she's introduced me to tonight."

"Wow." His lips remain in a surprised O.

"Yep."

"How do I fare in relation to the others?" He adopts a superman-like pose, and I can't help checking him out. If only he was wearing fitted spandex pants like a superhero. Then I could see what he's packing.

"Please take your time." His words cut into my ogling, and I bite back a smirk.

"I'm done. But I can't answer yet. It depends."

"On?"

"Your responses to a few well-crafted questions."

"Hit me. I'm game." He taps his chest and I almost reach out to do the same.

"Okay. One. Why are you here? In the US?"

"I'm on an athletic scholarship. My university back home offered an exchange program to improve our skills."

"Nice. And what skills would that be?"

"I have many." He bounces his eyebrows. "But the program is specifically for rugby."

"Rugby?" My eyes widen. "But you're at a hockey house."

"Good observation. My roommate is on the team."

"Ahh, gotcha."

"What's my next question?"

"How many women have you slept with since arriving?"

"None." He cringes and my face crinkles involuntarily. "I'm sensing that's not the answer you wanted, but it's an unfair question. I've only been here for a month."

"A month is a long time to go without sex." His face contorts, much like mine did, so I quickly add, "for some," and wink as though I'm joking. "Next question," I squeak out. "Do you know Penelope's cousin, Brant?"

"Ah, no. Should I?"

4

"Nope. That's a good answer. Last one. Have you heard any rumors about me?"

Jack frowns but he's quick to answer. "I didn't know who you were until about five seconds before Penelope shoved me your way."

"So...that's a no?"

"It is. Though now I'm curious." He quirks an eyebrow in question.

"No need to be." I smile innocently. "You passed the test."

"Great. What do I win?"

My lips twist and I try hard not to let my eyes drop to his body. "I haven't decided yet. Want to come and sit down?"

With a thoughtful gaze, Jack considers my question before letting out a short laugh and following me inside. "Lead the way. I'm seeing this through."

I'm laughing so hard, I snort obnoxiously, covering my mouth with my hand. "That's not real, is it? You don't *all* talk like that?"

"Try me," Jack challenges, raising a brow, making me smile at his boyish charm.

"Oh-kay. Give me a second to think."

He pauses when we reach the sorority house next to the hockey mansion, pulling me to a stop. Perhaps not wanting our time to come to an end.

We've been walking for the better part of an hour, chatting constantly, the smile barely leaving my face. In fact, we haven't stopped talking since Pen introduced us a few hours ago. There's something familiar about Jack. Despite us never previously meeting, we click. And that's rare for me.

Leaning against the white picket fence of the Alpha Kappa *whatever* house, I ponder Jack's challenge. Apparently, Australians can use the word "right" as a response to almost anything, and he wants to prove it.

"Got one. Did you know I'm auditioning for the role of Ophelia in a local production of *Hamlet* next month?"

"Yeah, right?" His tone lifts when he says "right" and I burst out laughing.

"Holy hell. It doesn't make any sense and yet it does."

"Told ya." He winks.

"Okay. What about this? I need help running lines, I—"

"Righto," he cuts in before I've finished my question.

"Right-oh?"

"Yep. I said what I said."

My laughter echoes through the quiet night air, and I half expect one of the sorority girls to come out and scold me. They're *not* the partying type. It's no accident their house borders the hockey team.

"You, Jack Bailey, are a funny fucker."

I've learned so much in the last few hours that it feels as though I've known him forever. It may be surface level for now, but something tells me there's more to Jack than meets the eye. And for some reason, I think I can trust him.

"Why, thank you." He gloats, flashing me a teasing grin. "I try. It's how I get the ladies."

"Riiight." I drag out the word and stare at him deadpan.

His jaw drops and his booming laughter follows. "Nailed it. I'll make an Aussie out of you yet."

"I'm looking forward to it. But back to you and the ladies. You know it's your abs, right?" I run my hands over the ridges apparent through his tight-fitting tee, following his V until I reach the waistband of his jeans.

"I do *now*," he rasps, shuddering slightly, his innocence a little endearing.

My phone rings before I can respond and I check the screen to find Pen calling.

"Excuse me a second," I say as I answer. "Pen?"

"Mike is here to pick us up. Are you coming or did I do good this time?" My eyes flash to Jack, and the shadow of his smirk tells me he can hear what she's saying.

"I think I'm going to stay out a little while longer. I'll get an Uber when I'm ready."

"Yes! I knew it. See you in the morning."

I hang up, and Jack's eyes lock on mine, a question in his gaze. A question I'm not sure I have the answer to. Because while I'm not at all ready to end our night together, I don't think it will end the way Pen assumes.

I have a feeling we're more likely destined to be friends. And I could use some more friends right now.

CHAPTER ONE
Jenna

EIGHT AND A HALF YEARS LATER

What the hell did I just read?

The letter feels strange in my hand as I flip it over, checking for a "just kidding" reference while pretending I can ignore the throbbing between my legs.

Jack's hinted at this side of himself. But the hints were so goddamn subtle I assumed I was imagining them. Wishful thinking on my part.

But this?

It's something straight out of a romance novel.

And I'm struggling to focus.

After meeting at the hockey team's Fourth of July party, Jack and I became close friends. Some would say we were inseparable for the following few months. But it was purely platonic. Jack's someone you file under the "too innocent for his good looks" category, and I wasn't going to be the one to corrupt him. As fun as that would have been.

He meant more to me than that. I liked having a male friend that didn't want to immediately get in my pants.

There were times I felt like he was the only one that truly knew me. Even my friendship with Penelope wasn't as deep, and I thought we told each other everything. Only I never opened up the way I did with Jack.

Life was good.

Until it all came to an abrupt end. Jack's time in the US ran short, and before I could process, he was on a flight back to Australia.

I can still remember our last conversation. I thought he was bullshitting me.

"I promise I'm not lying." Jack laughs as he speaks. "My coach needs me back there."

"That's what I'm not buying. If you'd said your family needs you...maybe I'd believe it."

"Fine. My family needs me." He bites back a smirk and I'm less convinced he's telling the truth. "Can I have your number? So we can keep in touch when I'm really gone?"

"Nope." I bite back a smile of my own. "You can have my address. I'll await your letters on the holidays."

Jack snorts but there's something about his expression that gives me pause.

"I'm happy to write you letters, Jenna. But I really am leaving." His smile softens before his face drops, and for the first time since he came barging into my room, announcing that he had to go home, my chest tightens.

"Riiight," I joke but my tone lacks humor. "You're leaving?"

"I am."

"For how long?"

"I don't know. I'll probably be back next semester." That's not too long.

"Okay, great. I guess you can have my number then." I reach for my phone until Jack stills my hand.

"I kind of like the letter idea."

"You what?" I laugh under my breath.

"How about I write to you for your Thanksgiving? Then you write back for Christmas."

I frown, my brows furrowing. That's a lot of work when we could text. "Come on." He bounces his eyebrows. "It will be fun."

"You're something else. You know that?"

"Yep. You love it."

"Okay. Fine. I want Valentine's Day to be included as a holiday. You can be my not-so-secret admirer."

"Done. But I'll be back by then." His wide smile warms my heart, but a nagging feeling settles in my chest, and I can't put my finger on what it is.

One thing's for sure. I'm going to miss him.

Jack never came back.

I was right. His Australian coach didn't need him. Why would he?

His family did.

His parents had been in an accident. They'd died. His coach didn't want to worry him for the fourteen-hour flight home since there was nothing he could have done.

Not that he told me that until we were two years into our letter exchange. He kept up the charade of his lie, until he was finally able to talk about it. Or write about it. He refused to give me his number, saying it was easier that way. And maybe he was right. Either way, our letters continued for eight years after he left.

Letters of friendship, support. Always innocent.

Until today.

God am I confused. And a little turned on.

Grabbing my phone, I shoot off a text to my friends, Blair and Hayley, hoping one of them is free to talk.

> **Me: Why the hell do my two closest friends live in San Francisco? I need you**

> **Blair: I've just walked in the door. Give me five and I'll call**

> **Me: Thank you. You're a godsend**

I breathe a sigh of relief and fall back to the couch, covering my face with my hands. Blair's my voice of reason. She's the Zen in my crazy-ass world. I have no doubt she'll ground me, because what I really want to do is board a plane to Australia and ask Jack what the hell is going on, while waving the letter in his face. I'm a live-in-the-moment kind of girl.

While I wait for her call, I read the letter again and my body heats. It's been a long time since someone surprised me in the bedroom, and if Jack can really do the things he says he wants to do... God damn. My core pulses just thinking about it. I'm taking this letter to bed with me later.

My phone buzzes across the table, pulling me out of my horniness as I rush to grab it.

> **Blair: Change of plans. I'm coming to LA. I've got two days off. What do you say we have a girls' weekend mid-week?**

My heart jolts. I really do have the best friends. Blair and I met last summer when she moved here with her douchebag ex. Now she lives in San Francisco with her new boyfriend. Or rather, her old boyfriend, after they reconnected a few months back. It sucks not having her here, but Zane is perfect for her, and since he plays for the San Francisco Storm football team, it made sense for her to move there.

Lucky for me, she visits often and I travel to San Francisco any chance I get.

> **Me:** Blair, I love you! How does Zane feel about that?

> **Blair:** It was *his* suggestion

> **Me:** Zane, my man. I knew I liked him

> **Blair:** I've got a few things to do tonight but I can be there by lunchtime tomorrow

> **Hayley:** Ooooh. I'm in LA too. I can meet you both for dinner tomorrow night. If that works?

And Hayley Jackman enters the conversation. Otherwise known as bestie number two. Though I would never rank them. They're equally amazing. Hayley's a big-name Hollywood actress, and also dating one of the guys from the Storm football team. But surprisingly, we didn't meet through Blair. I met Hayley on the set of a psychological thriller we starred in together. She had a guest role, and I was one of the regular cast—at least until they killed off my character.

While her star is much brighter than mine, Hayley and I became fast friends. She matches my crazy, yet she's down to earth and easy to get along with.

> **Me: Dinner sounds perfect. There's something I have to tell you both**

For some reason, I kept my friendship with Jack a secret from my friends. I guess I liked having something private in my life, while my world was constantly being picked apart and scrutinized.

Jenna Brooks steps out with another man after the premiere of her latest series.

TV star Jenna Brooks seen leaving the Prince Hotel at 4 a.m., on the arm of her recently divorced co-star.

Did Jenna Brooks sleep with one of the girls from Treasure Island? We've got an exclusive tell-all with the reality star.

The tabloids never bothered me—almost everything they reported had some truth to it. Still, I liked having a secret.

Now it's time to share the truth.

> **Hayley: Are you okay?**

> **Blair: You've got me worried**

> **Me: Thank you both. But I'm fine. It's a funny story. You're going to love it**

"**W**ait! You've been writing to each other multiple times *every* year for the past eight years?" Hayley's eyes widen as she stares at me in shock.

"Yep." I maintain my straight face while Hayley and Blair freak the hell out, both in their own special ways.

"And you never exchanged numbers?" Blair speaks slowly, perhaps giving her mind time to catch up. "Wow."

"I know, it's mind-blowing. Mostly because I bet neither of you thought I could commit to one person for that long. But it's the truth." *And now, he's fucking with my head.*

I'm questioning everything. Is he messing with me? Or does he want more? I'd firmly placed him in the friend zone with no thought of that changing. But now...a little part of me wants to find out. He was always so innocent. But it's been years. Maybe he's changed and wants to show me the real Jack.

"I love that he's Australian." Hayley interrupts my thoughts. "Your basic knowledge of my Aussie slang makes much more sense now."

"*Right?*"

She laughs heartily, while Blair's eyes bounce between the two of us. "Am I missing something?"

"Remind me to fill you in on Australians and their use of the word 'right.'"

"Okay." Blair shakes her head, her brows puckered until her expression morphs into one of excitement. "Back to the letters."

"Yes! Can we read them?" Hayley's face lights up, never one to hold back, while Blair's cheeks redden, most likely worried they're asking too much. I don't mind though.

"I've got nothing to hide. However, some of them are long. And the last one is going to surprise you."

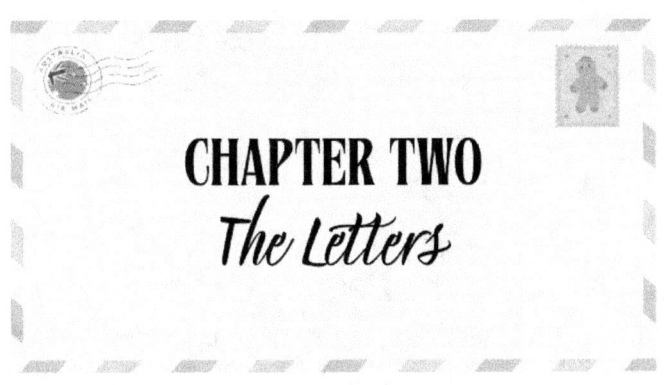

CHAPTER TWO
The Letters

EIGHT YEARS AGO

Dear Jenna,

G'Day and Happy Holiday season.

It's happening. Our first letter. You can now consider me your official pen pal.

And man, who knew letter writing would be this hard? This is my second attempt at writing something worth sending. I blame technology. Do you know how many times I grabbed my phone to text you? Until I remembered I stupidly decided this was a better idea. I'd insert an eye roll emoji here if I could bloody use them.

Anyway, moving on. Sorry, this is slightly later than expected. Some stuff happened back home that I wasn't expecting, and I needed a minute to focus on that.

I'm good now. You've just had Thanksgiving. A time to be grateful for the things we've got. Right? I wouldn't know since we don't celebrate it here. But I think I got the gist.

I'm thankful for you, by the way. My time in America may have been cut short, but God, I had fun while I was there. Even my brother says I'm not the same kid I was when I left Australia. And yep, he still calls me a kid. But he claims I've matured. A little. I still love video games and still can't hold my alcohol. But maybe you've made me wiser. I no longer do things because it's expected of me. I've started thinking for myself. Focusing on what I enjoy. Living in the moment. To a degree. And I have you to thank for that. So... Thank you.

How are you? How's Cali life? Is Pen still trying to set you up? Did you get the part you wanted in that local production? Or was that last month? I can't keep up. Now I believe it's your turn to respond, though I'm ninety percent sure you agreed as a joke and you're currently laughing at my expense. If you do respond, tell me the name of the park I got wasted in. The night you had to walk me home. That way, I know I'm not being catfished. You can never be too sure these days. I hope you have a great Christmas.

Cheers,

Jack

TWO YEARS LATER

Hi Jenna,

It always feels like too long between letters from Valentine's Day to Thanksgiving. Maybe you should add in another one. Halloween? Or something during the summer. That way, it's not a huge jump from one to the next.

Anyway, how are you?

Your last letter said you were counting down the days until graduation. Now you're out in the real world, and I have no idea what you're doing with your life. I won't even know if you got this.

On that note...did you get my graduation gift before you moved? I'm hoping it made it on time. If not, it was a care package for your new life as a "grown-up." It included a book about being an adult, some Advil, and your special hangover cure, because let's face it, it's going to be harder to bounce back when you have to go to work. Oh and a link to a playlist for your adulting adventures.

How is adult life anyway? Got any auditions coming up?

Life here is much the same as the last time we spoke. The team killed it this season. And we're favourites heading into the next season.

It's kind of taken over my life. I don't have time for much else.

Except when it comes to you. I'll always have time for this. I want to know everything. Fill me in. What does Jenna Brooks's life look like now? Are you on your way to stardom?

I look forward to hearing from you soon.

Take care,

Jack

THREE YEARS AFTER THAT

Jenna!!!!

How are you? Merry Christmas.

How's life back in Vermont? Did you go to the Christmas festival again this year? I've been thinking I should come and visit one day. I could deliver my letter in person. I'd love to have a white Christmas. Hell, by next year, I bet you'll be able to send a private jet to come and get me.

Which brings me to my next topic...

You did it!

I can't believe you're going to be on TV. For real. Well, I can believe it because you're one talented human, but I didn't think it would happen so soon. You hear stories about people waiting decades for their big break. And you've got yours.

Am I allowed to know what it is yet? I need to make sure we're getting it over here. Can you at least tell me what platform it's on? Anything? I'm proud of you, Jenna.

Now for my exciting news...

Oh that's right, I don't have any. But my bestie is going to be a huge star. Does that count? And yes, I mean you.

Anyway, hope you have a great break before your life changes beyond your wildest dreams. I'm pretty fucking excited that you've got the Valentine's Day letter this year. Your poem better be epic.

Talk soon.

Cheers,

Jack

PRESENT DAY

Jenna,

I'm going to assume my Thanksgiving letter was lost in the mail since you've never once missed a reply. But if that's not the case, you've got some explaining to do. Was it because I asked about your Mum—sorry MOM? Or is it because I laughed about your character being killed off in Piqued Interest? It was phenomenal acting but she was annoying as hell.

Even you admitted that.

If it was none of those things, I'm going to need you to tell me what it was, because it's driving me fucking insane. It's making me picture all the ways I could get back at you. And trust me...you do not want to peek inside this mind. I'm not sure our friendship could recover from that.

Imagine you found out that I wanted to bend you over my knee and slap your bare ass until it's red and raw, the outline of my handprint beautifully painting each cheek.

Actually, that wouldn't be a punishment for you, would it? No, I have no doubt you'd love that. You're probably throbbing right now.

The perfect punishment for you would be to make you lie face down on the bed, naked, with your glorious ass up in the air, your pussy on display for me. I'd trap your hands beside your head, maybe even blindfold you, messing with your senses.

Then I'd wait.

I might take my cock out. Make sure you hear my zipper sliding down. Torturously slowly. Leaving you to imagine what you'd see if I allowed you to look back.

But I wouldn't let you. Because that's exactly what you'd want.

You'd want to watch my cock slipping between your folds. You'd want to see your pussy sucking me in, taking me like the not-so-good girl that you are.

Sorry. That's not how this works. None of this is for you. It's all for me.

Because of that, I'd take my time, pumping my length as I watched you squirm, your pussy dripping in anticipation. And when I was ready, I'd run my hands all over your body, my fingers circling your centre, your clit, never once touching you where you needed it.

If you spoke, even so much as mewled, I'd stop. This is my payback after all.

How am I doing so far? Do you feel like you've paid your dues?

Personally, I think you need a little more.

How about I tease you until you can't hold back from screaming my name? Work you hard until you're begging for a release.

Maybe then I'd finally lean in and slowly run my tongue through your heat, lapping up your arousal. Maybe I'd suck your clit, give you everything you crave until you're seconds away from soaking my face.

Then I'd disappear. I'd leave you for a minute before coming back and doing it all again.

Edging you.

Over and over. Licking, sucking, plunging my fingers inside you.

And when you can't take any more, I'd...

It doesn't matter, I digress. I wasn't supposed to give you that insight.

If your letter did get lost along the way, I'm sorry for my outburst. I hope you have a wonderful Christmas. Got any grand plans? I'm having another quiet one this year but heading away in January. Me and a few of the guys are beach hopping up the coast. Should be fun.

Can't wait to hear all about your next project. You were auditioning for a feature film, right? You couldn't tell me the name but I think I recall it was an action comedy, and you were going to be a badass. The perfect role, I'd say.

Take care,

Jack

CHAPTER THREE
Jenna

"Holy shit. There is a lot to unpack here. You're right to be confused. That last letter. Phew! I'm burning up." Hayley fans her face, bouncing on the couch. We abandoned our half-eaten dinner as soon as the girls suggested reading the letters, and now we're spread out in my living room, letters all over the floor. "He was so innocent early on. And can I say, a little bit dorky?" She cringes and I try unsuccessfully to suppress my giggle.

"That's Jack. He still has his dorky moments."

"I like him," Blair adds, her cheeks a little more crimson than they were before she started reading what I'm calling Jack's "dirty" letter. "He seems sweet. But every now and then he changes. As though the real Jack was dying to come out and reveal himself, only he wasn't sure if he should."

"You think *that's* the real Jack? The last letter?"

"You don't?"

"I don't know. That's why I called for help." *Why I'm considering some drastic measures.*

Blair rubs at her forehead and we both turn to Hayley, hoping she has some great words of wisdom.

"What I love is that he actually edged you in that letter. I'm dying. What was he going to do next?"

"Right?!" That's why it made me so goddamn wet. I don't think I realized that he knew me that well. That intimately. "It's confusing. I'm confused."

"I'll bet. What are you going to write back?"

"I have no freaking idea."

"Why didn't you send him a Thanksgiving letter?" Blair asks, changing the topic. "If you've never missed a letter in eight years, why'd you miss that one? Was he right? Was it because he asked about your mom?" The concern etched into her features has me cringing. Trust her to focus on that part of the letter.

"Will you accept that I forgot?"

"Definitely not." She laughs gently, the concern still there.

"Me either." Hayley sides with Blair. "We may not have known you that long, but you're no flake."

Dammit. She's right. I'm no flake. And I didn't forget.

The truth is, my mom disappeared on me. *Again.* Just when I was getting used to having her around.

I was looking forward to another white Christmas in Vermont. Counting down the days. I'm not due to start my next project until January. The timing was perfect. She'd promised it would be the two of us this year, and it's been years since that happened.

Sure, I'm an adult now. Old enough to have my own kids if that's what I wanted. Only, what I want is my mom. I shouldn't be letting her get to me so much, but every time she walks back into my life, promising me that she's done with the shitty men in hers, I believe it. And every time, she finds another douchebag and makes him her whole world, leaving me behind.

Forgetting she has a daughter.

It's been that way since my dad died. In the past, she claimed that she needed someone to help take care of me. Because she was always in and out of work. But I moved to LA when I was eighteen. She can't use that excuse nine years later.

You'd think I'd be used to it by now. And I should be. Only this time, she disappeared to France, leaving her landlord my details to collect rent.

I wanted to write to Jack. But with that, and everything that happened with Blair and Zane these past few months, I wasn't in the right headspace. The last thing he needs is me complaining about the drama with my mom during the holiday season when his parents are dead. At least I've got a parent in my life.

"If I tell you, you're not allowed to feel sorry for me, or harp on about it. Our focus today is Jack and his latest letter, not what I'm about to say."

Hayley nods, while Blair hesitates. "Um. I—"

"I never pushed you to talk about your past," I remind her and she blows out a breath.

"Okay. Deal."

"Thank you."

I fill them in on my upbringing and the latest shit show with my mom, and Hayley gives me the response I was after. "God, some parents suck."

"That they do."

Hayley's told me a bit about her parents back in Australia, so I know she understands a little of what I'm going through. Blair's parents, on the otherhand, are amazing. I've only met them once, but I would love for them to adopt me like they've all but adopted Zane.

Blair's quiet, and when I glance over, she's sucking her lips into her mouth, her watery eyes highlighting the depth of her sadness. For me.

And now I feel bad.

"Okay. Get it over with."

"Oh, Jenna." She leaps up from her seat and rushes over to give me a hug. "Hayley's right; some parents *do* suck and I'm sorry you were dealt a shitty hand."

"Thank you."

"Is there anything we can do to help? How about you come to Jacksonville for Christmas with my family?"

I cringe at the thought, and wish I'd seen her invite coming because I would have hidden my involuntary response. "As wonderful as that sounds, I'm okay." I had a short fling with Blair's brother and would prefer to avoid him if I can. It's not that we ended badly or anything. It was casual sex and we both knew that. But he joked about us "doin' it again sometime" and that's not what I do. "I'm actually thinking of getting away. Maybe heading abroad."

I smile innocently, but they both see right through it. "Oh my God," Hayley squeals while Blair's hand flies to her face with her gasp.

"You're going to Australia?" she questions, her jaw parting in surprise.

"Australia? I hadn't really decided on a location. Australia could be nice. It's summer, right, Hayls?"

"It is." Her lips purse as she suppresses a smile. "Christmas is the perfect time to visit."

"Well, I mean, if you're both suggesting it." I shrug and Blair snorts out a laugh.

"Come on. What are you going to do? Confront Jack?"

"That's exactly what I was thinking. You can't send a letter like that and expect me to do nothing."

"He was probably expecting you to write back. I'm sure he guessed, rightly so, that it would get a rise out of you."

"A rise? Oh B, if I was a guy, my cock would have been at full mast while reading that letter. And Jack knows me, meaning he knew exactly what he was doing. The more I say it aloud, the more I think I need to confront him."

"Yes!" Hayley cheers. "I am so here for this."

"I don't know." Blair hesitates. "What are you going to say?"

"I'm going to knock on his door and ask him to explain himself."

Hayley's smile widens. "Please tell me you're also planning on screwing his brains out?"

"I'm considering it."

"Nooo." Blair shakes her head vehemently. "What if you sleep together and it ruins your friendship?"

"You have a point. We'll have to set ground rules."

"That doesn't work." Hayley leans forward, her expression pinched. "Reed and I tried. The boundaries make it more enticing."

"Hmm. It does give it a forbidden feel."

"Exactly."

"What if you're soulmates?" Blair blurts suddenly, silencing us both.

"What?" Laughter bubbles out of me and I shake my head. "He's not my soulmate."

"How do you know? I tried really hard to pretend Zane wasn't my forever, and look how that turned out. Think about it. You tell each other everything. The banter is on point. He obviously likes you, and the fact that you continue to respond means that you like him too."

"Oh," Hayley cuts in. "Yes. I can see that. The final letter is him shooting his shot."

"By telling me all the dirty things he wants to do to me?"

"Yes. It shows how well he knows you. The key to your heart is through your clit."

"Hayley!" Blair scolds jokingly, failing to hold back her laughter.

"Am I wrong?" Hayley gloats, a sassy smile pulling at her lips.

"Nope. You're spot on. That's why I'm still single. I haven't found anyone that knows the exact way I like my clit serviced. My hand is still number one."

Blair scoffs, determination set in her brow. "I don't believe that. You haven't settled down because you haven't found someone that sets your heart on fire. Someone you think about twenty-four seven. A guy or girl who knows everything about you because they pay attention, not because you told them. Because you're their entire world and they'd do anything to make you happy."

I stare at her for a beat, rolling her words around in my mind. Is that true? Is that what I'm waiting for? An image of Jack's letter comes back to mind and I shake off my thoughts.

"Nah. It's definitely the pleasure I'm missing."

Hayley erupts into laughter while Blair sighs dramatically.

"Can you at least wait until you have it all before you settle?"

"Does that actually exist?"

"Yes!" They cry out in unison, and I rear back from the outburst.

"God, you're both so loved up it's nauseating. But I can't deny that you have great men. For you."

Hayley smiles brightly while Blair glances away, seemingly lost in thought. My brows furrow, patiently waiting until she nods a few times and turns back to face us.

"Okay. I've mentally weighed the pros and cons while we've been talking, and I think you should go to Australia."

My lips twist in amusement and I gesture for her to elaborate. "I'm listening."

I've all but made up my mind, but it can't hurt to cement my decision. Blair is the queen of pros and cons lists, and I have no doubt it will be well thought out.

She raises a finger, her face creasing into a proud smile. "One, it would be cool to experience Christmas in Australia. Two, if you're planning an escape either way, then at least you'll be around someone you know. Three, I heard the chocolate there tastes incredible and that's reason enough in itself."

While the first two are take it or leave it, she has a good point about the third. I'd go anywhere for incredible chocolate.

"Four," she continues and I bite back a smile, "your favorite swimwear brand has a physical store there, somewhere on the east coast. If it's close, you'll be able to pop in and try on the different styles."

"B! I hadn't thought of that. Even if it's not close, I'm going to have to visit."

"Yes! Ugh, I'm jealous. There are so many amazing stores in Australia that you don't get here. Mainly beachwear." Hayley starts naming a few brands until Blair stops her.

"What if they're all in different states?" she asks, always the practical one.

"He's in Sydney, right?" Hayley turns my way. "I think he mentioned that in one of his letters."

"That's right."

"Well, you're in luck, as most of the ones I know are in Sydney."

"Perfect, it's settled. I'll go shopping first and stock up on swimsuits and summer outfits ahead of my beachy vacation."

"Does Jack live near the beach?"

"He sure does. He described it to me in one of his earlier letters, maybe one you didn't read. Though, I guess he could have been lying this whole time. We'll soon find out." I laugh and Hayley joins in while Blair merely smiles, and there's something off about it.

"What's wrong?"

"I missed something on my cons list."

"Oh, yeah?"

"What if he's been lying to you this whole time?" She repeats my words back to me, but while I was joking, she's definitely not.

"Oh, B. I'm a big girl. I can handle myself."

"*And* if that is true, you bet your ass I'm boarding the next flight out of here to help you kick his ass," Hayley adds, her expression murderous but adorable, if that's possible.

"Thanks, Hayls." I smile warmly and turn to Blair. "Thank you both. I appreciate you helping me through this. Good list, Blair."

"I actually have one more."

"Wow, you are on fire." Hayley squeezes her arm.

"I do these a lot."

"Let's hear it."

"Okay. Five, Jack might be your soulmate."

I laugh, a little hysteria in my voice, as Hayley snorts beside me. "B, I swear you weren't this corny when you were dating Nathan."

"Then look at what finding your soulmate does. It turns the pessimists into optimists again."

"If that's the case, I'm going to make it my life's goal to avoid mine." I wink as though I'm joking, only I'm not sure that I am.

"Stop." Blair manages a small, tentative smile. "You love it. But just in case, do you want to hear the rest of the cons?"

CHAPTER FOUR
Jenna

T he smell of salt permeates the air as I enter Jack's beautiful tree-lined street, and when I come to a stop in front of his house, my jaw drops. Not only does he live *one* street away from the beach in the most gorgeous town I think I've ever driven through, but his house could grace the cover of a home design magazine.

The modern glass and painted concrete structure sits back off the street, behind a perfectly manicured garden and lawn. It's two...no, three stories high, and... Holy shit, is that a pool on the second level?

While the topic of money never came up in our letters, I got the feeling his parents had been well-off. But I wasn't expecting this. It doesn't fit his personality. He's carefree and fun and not at all organized enough to keep this place in check. Even if he's paying a housekeeper to help. It's not him.

Though, come to think of it, he hasn't moved since the first letter he sent me. This could very well be his parents' house. The house he grew up in.

If I grew up in a house like this, in this location, I wouldn't move either.

God, I have so many questions. And that means it's time to get the fuck out of the car to get answers.

Closing my window, I adjust my oversized sunglasses and grab my phone to leave, pausing when it vibrates in my hand.

> **Blair: I've changed my mind. Come home. What if he's a psycho?**

My laughter bellows and I wish Blair was here so I could reach out and hug her. It's been eighteen hours since I last spoke to her and three days since I made the decision to come. Yet she chooses now, when I'm in front of his house, to change her mind. Oh, B.

My phone buzzes again, and I smile at Hayley joining the chat.

> **Hayley: He's not a stranger, Blair. Jenna's met him**

> **Blair: Eight years ago. People change**

> **Me: Some do. Some really don't**

> **Me: I'm already parked in front of his house, seconds away from getting out of the car**

After puckering my lips, I touch up my gloss and grab the door handle, until another message comes through.

> **Blair: Wait! I've added to my cons list and I thought you should know**

> **Blair: Cons—He could be a psycho. He might have an awful haircut (Hayley showed me photos of some popular Australian styles and just...no. You are better than that), and finally, he may be all talk and no action**

An obnoxious laugh snorts out of me and I cover my mouth with my hand.

> **Hayley: Ooh she's right. He could be rocking a long-haired mullet**

An image follows showing a guy with a unique haircut that could rival something from the eighties, and I shudder at the sight. *That's got to be fake.* I hope. But real or not, I'm confident in saying...

> **Me: He doesn't have a mullet**

At *least he didn't.* Eight years ago.

The Jack I remember had short hair, almost a buzz cut, and a rigid jaw line. He was also, as Blair said, a little bit nerdy. He doesn't strike me as the type of guy to have a mullet. But... people *do* change. Hell, I've changed since we first met. I was a platinum blonde with stick-straight hair back then. Now I keep my hair natural—light brown with soft waves.

Makes me wonder why we never exchanged more recent photographs over the years. Although, I'm on TV and Jack's a professional rugby player—*Rugby*, not league. I have no idea what that means but he was always sure to distinguish between the two. Either way, I'm sure I could find his photo online.

Hayley: You could look him up

I laugh at her thoughts reflecting my own, only I have a better option, now that I'm here.

Me: Or...I could just knock on his door?

Hayley: Yes, go get him, girl

Blair: Be careful

If I wasn't as convinced as I am that I know him, I'd probably be worried like Blair, but I'm not. I'd be willing to bet he's the same guy he is in his letters. Except maybe the last letter because that's a whole different side of him that I never knew existed. I can't wait to meet him.

God, if he—

A thundering knock startles me and I throw my phone, watching it disappear between the seat and the center console. *Goddammit. What the hell was that for?* Armed with an obviously forced smile, I turn to greet the shadowy figure lurking by my window—ready to give them a piece of my mind—but freeze at the sight of him.

Hot *damn*. Are all Australians gorgeous? I should have made the trip sooner.

My smile turns real until I register the curl of his lips, and the anger in his eyes throws me. *What did I do?*

"Move your car!" He answers my unspoken question, gesturing for me to move out of my prime parking space and pointing down the road. "This is not beach parking."

The beach? That's not why I'm here. Not entirely. According to B, I'm here to meet my soulmate, and this guy is ruining my buzz.

"What?" I mouth, pointing to my ear, pretending I can't hear him. "I'm sorry." I frown sympathetically, hoping to get a rise, and he delivers with the most delicious scowl.

His nose flares, frustration rising, and I almost laugh but catch myself in time.

"Open the window," he yells, tapping on the glass, seemingly believing I can't hear him. *Was he born yesterday?*

I roll my eyes even though he can't see them, and do as he asked, smiling while the window opens. "Can I help you?" I lower my sunglasses ever so slightly and innocently bat my eyelashes.

The guy's eyes widen before he shakes his head in annoyance. "You need a permit to park here."

"I'm sorry, are you a cop?"

"No. I live here." He says no in that long way Aussies say it—nawr or noowa—and it makes me smile, further pissing him off.

"The fun police then? Got it. I'll risk the ticket." I grab the door handle, as his fingers curl around the windowsill, the veins in his tanned skin bulging.

And *fuck me*...I'm moving here. I don't need to be a Hollywood star. I'll be a beach babe. I'll—

"Move your *damn* car." His hand tightens around the metal and I struggle to avert my gaze. *I wonder if he realizes the anger makes him hotter.* "Look, I just got home from a long night at work."

"So...?"

"You need a permit to park here!"

"Oooh. You want my *parking space?*"

"Yes!"

"Can't you park somewhere else? Don't you have a driveway?"

"I do but I can't park there because... God. I don't have to explain myself. I need you to move your car."

"Where am I going to park?"

"Not my problem."

"It kind of is. I'm not going to move until I know where to go."

"God—" He cuts himself off and steps back, running a hand down his gorgeous face, his expression turning neutral. "*Please*. Can you please move your car so I can park here? The inspectors come by at least three times a day. Trust me, you don't want that fine."

My shoulders drop along with the tone of his voice, and I let out a soft sigh. "Okay. I'm going."

"Thank you."

He walks away without another word and I search around for my phone, taking one last look at Jack's house before throwing my rental into drive and pulling away. I resist the urge to flip him off, but when it takes me another twenty-five minutes to find somewhere that isn't marked with a residents only sign, I regret that decision. At least then I'd have an ounce of satisfaction to accompany my frustration.

I'm a hot mess by the time I make it to Jack's front door, and only then does it occur to me that he may not be home. *Why the hell didn't we exchange goddamn phone numbers?*

I knock on the huge gray door until I find what appears to be an intercom and buzz the doorbell. A red light comes on and I smile, certain that something *that* fancy has a camera.

I almost wave until the door flies open and I jump, coming face-to-face with someone that is definitely *not* Jack.

Instead, the broody god from the street stands dripping in front of me, an obnoxiously bright beach towel wrapped around his waist. Water pools in the crevices of his abs, and I find myself watching one little drop as it makes its way toward his—

"Can I help you?" He clears his throat, repeating my words back to me. I continue to stare at his chest, the answer yes sitting on the tip of my tongue.

I bet he could help me *goood.*

My body heats, imagining all the things he could do to me.

"Jenna?"

I snap out of my fantasy, my gaze darting to Jack standing behind my new "friend," finding him in a similar state of undress, only, he's somehow more alluring since he's wearing gray sweatpants and an adorably confused expression. Much better than a scowl.

"Holy fucking shit." His face splits into a wide grin. "I'm in shock. Jenna Brooks is standing on my doorstep. What are you doing here?"

"I was in the neighborhood and—"

"No way, really?" His eyes grow and a laugh escapes me.

"No. I got your Christmas letter and decided to come and explain myself in person." *While also seeking answers on what the hell your letter was about.*

"You did?" Surprise registers on Jack's face, and his eyes briefly flash to the guy holding the door.

"I did."

He frowns, and for the briefest of seconds, I wonder if I made a mistake. Until I remember I'm in Australia. What do I care if he tells me to fuck off—there's plenty for me to do. And I don't just mean activities.

I raise a questioning brow, and Jack's expression morphs until he's smiling in awe. "Sorry. As I said, I'm in shock. I can't believe you're here. At my house. In Australia. Bro, can you believe it?" He turns to look at the gorgeous grumpy asshole again, and it's then I see the resemblance. "It's Jenna, bro. The girl I've been writing to for *years*. Jenna, this is my brother, Mason."

Before I can respond, Mason looks my way again, his grayish-blue eyes appraising me with dislike. "The infamous pen pal," he says, sounding bored. "I'll leave you two to...whatever." He shrugs, turning away.

"I believe the description you're looking for is 'catch up.'"

Mason glances back at me and sneers, releasing the door and walking away as it closes in my face, forcing Jack to rush forward to grab it.

"Sorry." Jack cringes. "He's pissed off because I made him answer the door when he'd just jumped into the pool."

"The one on your balcony?"

"No." Jack frowns again as though that's a preposterous idea and gestures behind him. "The one out back."

"Oh, *riiight*." I wink with a grin and Jack chuckles, the sound of it bringing me back to our time together in college. Like nothing has changed.

"I still can't believe you're here." His awe returns and I feel good about my decision to come.

"Surprise." I wave my hands around. "But...are you going to invite me in?" I raise a brow, and he curses, chuckling to himself.

"Fuck, yes. Come in. Come in. You actually came on a good day. We're having a pool party with some friends. You brought bathers, right?"

"Bathers?" A soft giggle escapes me, remembering how much shit I gave Hayley for using that term. "I did. A pool party sounds fun."

He smiles brightly and my heart jolts, a warmth spreading through me that I haven't felt before. I smile back but shake off my thoughts the second he turns to guide the way. *Dammit, Blair.* He is *not* my soulmate.

Soulmates don't exist.

CHAPTER FIVE
Mason

I nurse a beer, pretending to listen while my best friend, Kai, complains about our boss, Livvy, my gaze locked on the pool behind him. Or more specifically, my brother's shiny new toy. He's like a kid on Christmas. If emoji came to life, he'd have goddamn heart eyes.

Kai scoffs louder than necessary, drawing my attention and I frown, nodding my head in solidarity, though I have no idea what he said. He's been trying to win Livvy over since I got him the bartending job at my work three years ago. But she's never once wavered from her "I don't fuck my employees" rule. Until now. And it wasn't Kai.

"What does Chris have that I don't?" he asks when I'm finally looking his way, and I huff out a laugh.

"You mean, other than the fact that he has model good looks and the reputation of a sex god?"

"The fuck, Mase?"

I chuckle as his face contorts. "I'm kidding. They've known each other since high school. It's possible she already had a thing for him when she hired him."

"How the hell do you know that?"

"Livvy."

"You talk to her?"

"You don't?"

"Not really."

"Then how... You know what? It doesn't matter." I hold back an incredulous laugh, stopping short of shaking my head. Other than Livvy, Kai usually has his pick of the ladies—his words, not mine. And yet, he's clueless when it comes to women. It constantly blows my mind.

"What do you think of your brother's new girl?" He changes the subject, leering at Jenna when she sashays past. "She looks familiar." He squints as though that will ignite something in his brain, and I give him a shove so he'll stop staring.

"She's not my brother's girl," I grate, moving in front of him, forcing him to look at me instead of the Brazilian-style bikini riding up her ass.

"Are you sure?" Kai nods his head toward my brother who is practically drooling from the edge of the pool.

"She's the pen pal."

"No. Fucking. Way. That's where I know her. I binged that superhero series." Kai shoves me aside to perve on her again, and I spin to watch as she grabs another drink, shaking her hips to the music. With the way she's dancing, you'd think she'd known everyone for years, but we're lucky if it's been three hours. She's *that* confident in herself.

"I can't believe she's here," Kai continues. "I was sure he was making her up."

"Ha. Same." Not really, but I never once expected her to turn up on our doorstep. Jack must have asked me a million times if I could believe it. And the truth is, I can't.

Jenna waltzes back to Jack, her smile flirtatious as she lowers herself to the edge of the water. She takes a sip of her drink, and the second she puts it aside, Jack pulls her into the pool, eliciting a squeal that makes me cringe.

"They're definitely going to fuck," Kai puts his two cents in, and the urge to punch him is strong. He can be an annoying motherfucker, but I don't usually want to hurt him.

What the fuck is going on? And when will this party be over?

Needing a reprieve, I make myself comfortable in our cabana, lying back on a lounge chair farthest from the pool. Then I adjust my position, making sure the obnoxious half-naked mermaid sculpture—that Jack insisted on buying—blocks my view.

As the afternoon sun peaks, the conversation turns to Christmas, with our cousin Roxy reminding everyone it's her turn to host our annual Boxing Day celebration. Excitement fills the air but I'm not feeling it, despite usually being all in for this tradition.

I'm sure once we all grow the fuck up—and some of us have kids—it'll fizzle out, but for now, it's the only celebration Jack and I get. We spend Christmas day together if one of us isn't working, and we always exchange gifts, but it's not the big deal it was when we were kids. When our parents were around.

And I love Christmas.

I tried hard to keep our personal traditions going for the first few years after we lost Mum and Dad, but when Jack made it clear he didn't want that, I gave up the fight.

"The drinks will be flowing and the food will be five star," Roxy announces, changing things up from our usual BBQ and beer. "I'm going for a Hawaiian theme, so you better be ready for fruity cocktails and seafood galore. And Santa. Christmas wouldn't be the same if we didn't have photos on Santa's lap. A more traditional one than last year. Thanks, Kai."

Kai raises his beer in the air. "Anytime. You all loved it."

Every year, the girls hire some gorgeous model to be Santa, and he always happens to forget his shirt, turning up in an open jacket. But last year, it was Kai's turn to host and Santa was replaced with Mrs. Claus. The late twenties version. And God, was she smoking hot.

Someone wolf whistles and I lean forward, turning toward the sound, finding Jack laughing while Jenna smiles uncomfortably beside him. She forces a giggle at something he says before jumping up and heading inside, returning with a full bottle of vodka in hand—and no glasses. My stomach knots as she whispers to Jack, a lopsided grin lighting up his face.

And it pisses me off. *Can't he see that something's wrong?* She's clearly upset, and I'm going to go out on a limb and say she's about to drink herself stupid because of it.

After spending the next hour *not* watching Jack and Jenna knock back shots directly from the bottle, I jump up, needing to escape.

Jenna's not my problem, and Jack's a grown-ass man—he can take care of himself. I don't need to worry about either of them.

And I'm not. I'm fine.

The second I leave the lounge chair, Roxy pounces on it, poking her tongue out when I raise an eyebrow in question. "What? You haven't moved for hours," she whines, "and Kai's got the other one. Stevie and I need to sit down."

"Good luck with that." I chuckle, gesturing to Kai asleep on the lounge. That guy can sleep anywhere, and he worked the night shift last night. He's not budging.

Roxy's eyes sparkle with mischief and before I know it, she's pushing Kai off the lounge, thankfully in the direction of the grass.

"What the fuck, Rox?" Kai glares as he jumps up until his eyes lock on Roxy's friend, Stevie, and his anger instantly dissipates. "Hello, *Red*." He bounces his eyebrows. "I don't think we've officially met."

Stevie brushes her red hair behind her ear and playfully rolls her eyes. "Red? How original."

I scoff under my breath and leave them to it, ducking around Roxy as she crosses her arms over her chest, ready to protect her friend. Kai's a good guy, but he's the definition of a playboy, and from what Roxy's told me about Stevie, he's not her type.

But at least he's forgotten about Livvy. For the time being anyway.

If only I could forget about *my* current fixation.

As if reading my mind, Jenna laughs as I pass her and Jack on my way to the kitchen, and I internally groan. But when the tightness in my chest eases, I'm forced to admit I may have been a little more worried than I realized. As I'm sure she expected—since she grabbed the bottle of vodka herself—the alcohol seems to have worked to erase whatever was troubling her. And while I'm not condoning drinking your issues away, I'm relieved to see her happy again. Either that, or she's numb.

Is she numb? Is that it? I pause—God knows why—but thankfully catch myself without drawing attention. *Keep walking, Mason. They don't need you. She doesn't need you.*

Smiling at no one in particular, I continue on my way, grabbing a glass from the cabinet in the kitchen, filling it with water. Cloud cover momentarily darkens the sky as I stare out the window, my drink forgotten while I search the yard. For what? I don't know.

Kai cannonballs into the pool, drenching Rox and Stevie, and while I feel bad for them, an uncontrollable burst of laughter escapes me.

I'm going to guess he did not get Stevie's number. He's—

"I think that's the first time I've heard you genuinely laugh. It always has an edge to it." I jolt at Jenna's sudden appearance but recover quickly, spinning around to face her.

"Always?" I scoff. "In the five hours you've known me?"

"That's right. You can tell a lot about a person the first time you meet them."

"Is that so?"

"Yep. Which reminds me." She raises her hands like she's under arrest, and her tiny bikini top shifts, the base of her tits peeking out from below.

My traitorous cock twitches.

"What are you doing?" I rush out, keeping my eyes on her face. I'm not blind; she's fucking gorgeous, but she's also sassy and annoying. Not to mention she's off-limits. Reserved for my baby brother. And what baby bro wants, baby bro gets.

Jenna bites her lips mockingly before batting her eyelids. "Don't arrest me, fun police. I promise I'm bored out of my mind right now. Nothing to see here." She puts on an innocent tone that sounds a lot like Dorothy from *The Wizard of Oz* and I huff under my breath.

"You're hilarious," I deadpan. "I hope you found a parking spot."

"I did, thank you. It's just a short fifteen-minute walk from here." She smiles, but the annoyance in her expression warms my heart.

"Good."

"Good?" She huffs like I did, although hers is more cheerful than mine. "You're really something."

"That I am."

Her smile returns as she shakes her head, and when I spin to empty the water I never drank, she falls quiet, drawing my gaze in the window reflection.

"You have a nice house," she says softly, surprising me. "It's so clean and inviting."

"Clean and inviting?" I bite back a sarcastic laugh and glance over my shoulder. She's a little tipsy so I'll let that one slide.

"Yes, clean and inviting. Not at all what I expected for Jack, and after spending the last few hours getting reacquainted, that opinion hasn't changed."

"Oh-kay." *What's she getting at?*

"This is all you. Isn't it?"

"What?" My brows raise of their own accord, though she's not far off base. My dad may have designed this place—he was a renowned architect—and my mum may have furnished it, but for the past eight years, I've made it a home. How Jenna could possibly know that after spending five minutes in my presence is beyond me.

"Am I wrong?"

"We share the house." I shrug, not knowing how else to respond.

"Oh, I know. But I'm willing to bet you don't share responsibilities."

"Do you need something?" I change the subject, not at all interested in a deep and meaningful conversation.

"Another bottle?" Jenna points to the empty bottle of vodka on the bench beside her and I cringe, biting back a remark. She's not my problem, I remind myself. She doesn't need me telling her what she can and can't do, though my head is screaming at me to beg her to slow down. To be careful. She doesn't know these people. Hell, she doesn't know me. Or Jack. Outside of his letters.

"Do...you...know where I can find one?" she enunciates slowly when I don't respond. "Jack mentioned—"

"Yep. Above the fridge."

"Thanks." Her smile brightens and she reaches up again, but this time I turn away, avoiding the peep show, refusing to look back until she's gone.

When the party dies down a few hours later, I'm already inside when Jack stumbles in, his arm wrapped around Jenna's shoulder as she whispers in his ear. Giggling.

She pauses when she spots me, her deep brown eyes raking over me, her bottom lip trapped between her teeth. It's so goddamn seductive that I bite back a groan.

"I'm taking Jenna to bed," Jack tells me, oblivious to her ogling. "She'll be in the room across from mine."

I nod, sucking in a breath as he guides her up the stairs, and it's not until he returns a few minutes later that I finally relax. *Thank fuck.* He didn't take advantage of her. I shouldn't have doubted him. He's a better guy than I give him credit for. But still... If that had been Kai...I wouldn't have held back from kicking his ass.

"I'm going to get her some painkillers and water," he says, heading toward the kitchen. "Jenna's going to have the mother of all hangovers when she wakes in the morning." He laughs, while my insides churn.

"Aren't you worried about her?" She wasn't drinking that much until the conversation turned to Christmas. And she loves Christmas. At least that's what I was led to believe.

Jack frowns, tossing his head in nonchalance. "She's always been the life of the party. Remember she told me about that festival back home in Vermont? She was so drunk, she woke up in the sleigh from a Christmas display." He laughs again, and the knot in my stomach tightens.

What do both events have in common? Christmas. My eyes flash to the stairs and I school my features, hiding my concern.

"You're probably right. I don't know her like you do."

"Not even close, big bro." He winks and I force a half-assed smile. "I'm gonna grab Jenna's stuff and head off to bed. I need my beauty sleep for the big day I have planned tomorrow."

"Big day?"

"Yep. I'm taking Jenna out. Showing her the sights Sydney has to offer."

"It's going well then?"

"So fucking good. It's like old times. You'd think no time had passed."

I clench my teeth as I hold my grin. "Good to hear, man. Good to hear."

He walks away and my chest burns, but I refuse to acknowledge what that means. She's Jenna. Jack's Jenna. And that's all she'll ever be.

CHAPTER SIX
Jenna

My head throbs behind my eyes and a groan rumbles from my throat. I'm not ready to wake up. Covering my face, I prepare for the brightness to attack me, but it's surprisingly dark and not at all as bad as I expected. The smell of coffee permeates the air as I fumble around for my phone, checking the time with a frown. Nine a.m. How is it dark? And where the hell am I?

Vague flashes of dancing and laughter dart through my mind and my head catches up. Jack walked me to bed last night. I can't remember everything that happened, but that fact is clear as day. Because I panicked. I'm not someone that turns a guy down if we've been having fun together—and Jack was a blast. Only, just like back in our sophomore year, my gut instinct told me not to go there. Not yet anyway. No matter how often I think about his last letter, talking to him reminds me of the innocent guy he was back in college. My *friend*. It turns out, I'm not ready to fuck that up.

The ache in my head turns to a pounding when I try to sit up, but as I rub my temples, my eyes lock on the nightstand and my heart races.

He remembered.

A smile tugs at my lips and I spin around, taking the tablets left out for me and gulping back the energy drink. A moan escapes me as the grape-flavored goodness flows down my throat. Who knew Jack was so thoughtful?

Even more of a reason *not* to fall into bed with him.

My smile widens as I imagine Blair marking this down on her pros list. *He knows your favorite hangover cure. He must be my soulmate.*

Soft music filters in from somewhere in the house and I laugh to myself. There will be no thoughts of soulmates today. Jack is a friend. Nothing more. It's time to get my ass up out of bed.

After a quick shower—in the bathroom conveniently located across from my room—followed by minimal effort getting ready, I make my way downstairs, beelining for the kitchen. *I'm in desperate need of some food.*

Jack's waiting when I reach the bottom step, his warm smile bringing about my own. "Good morning. How did you sleep?"

"Like a log."

"Good." He chuckles lightly. "And...how did you wake up?" He cringes and it's my turn to giggle.

"Waking up was a bitch, but I feel better thanks to you. The Advil, or whatever you call it, and energy drink worked wonders. I can't believe you remembered that."

"Energy drink?" Jack frowns, glancing away in thought, and my mind whirs.

"Yeah." I hesitate. "You left it out for me. Didn't you?"

The furrows in his brow deepen before he barks out a deep laugh. "I didn't think I was *that* drunk last night, but my memory seems to be a little sketchy. I'm glad I remembered in my drunken state, and I'm happy it helped."

"You're still a lightweight then?" I bite my lip to stifle a smile and Jack winces dramatically.

"Maybe. Though...you were making me drink vodka straight from the bottle."

"Very true. I'm surprised you were walking let alone able to escort me to my room."

"Me too." His belly rumbles in a chuckle, as Mason clears his throat from down the hall, drawing my gaze. I hadn't noticed he was standing there.

"Oh, fuck." Jack winces again. "I was waiting here for a reason. How would you like to spend the day exploring Sydney with me?"

"I'd love that."

"Great." Jack turns to Mason, giving him a cheesy grin. "Soo..." he begins, eliciting a deep huff from Mason.

"Fine. But you better not crash it."

"I had *one* accident and you've never let it go." He turns back to face me. "It wasn't even bad."

I snort under my breath and I swear Mason groans. I may have no idea what's going on, but I love good sibling banter. Probably because I never had siblings of my own. *I wanted that.*

"Don't forget about the ground rules, baby bro." Mason stares pointedly and I enjoy that too. He's cute when he's grumpy. "My keys are by the door," he grates, disappearing out of sight.

"In case you haven't figured it out, we're taking Mase's car. Mine is..." Jack trails off with an awkward shrug.

"Disgusting," Mason calls out, making me giggle behind my hand. "That's what it is."

"Disgusting, huh?"

Jack winces but confirms with a nod. "Yep. I could take better care of it. But I don't."

"Okay. Where are we going?" I change the subject, silently adding car cleanliness to Jack's cons list, while his face lights up, embarrassment gone.

"It's a surprise."

"Do I need a bikini?"

"Not this morning, but maybe later today."

"Great. Can I eat first or—"

"I'm taking you out for a greasy breakfast."

I moan loudly at the thought, my mouth watering at the idea of bacon, until a loud clang brings me back to reality.

"You okay, bro?" Jack calls out, a brow raised in amusement. "*Fine.*"

"Okay, then." I smile at Jack, spinning on my toes. "I'll grab my purse."

Jack opens my door when we get to Mason's car, and my smile grows at finding it in the same spot I was refusing to vacate. God, he's a douche. I mentally roll my eyes, but when I sit down, his masculine scent assaults my nostrils, and my body heats against my will. *Damn him.* He rubs me the wrong way, but I can't deny that I'm physically attracted to him.

"Are you ready?" Jack smiles giddily from the driver's seat.

"I sure am."

There's also no denying Jack's attractive too, but they are two completely different people. I could easily fuck Mason and move on, but with Jack... I'd either break his heart, or he'd break mine, because our friendship wouldn't be the same after. It may only be a few letters a year, but he's been the one constant in my life since college. That's not something I'm prepared to risk for sex.

Pushing my thoughts out of my mind, I stare out the window, drinking it all in as we cruise the streets of Sydney. "Where are we going for breakfast? Or I guess it's brunch now."

A siren blares through Jack's speakers, making me jump as he curses. "Shit. That's my phone."

"Your phone?" *What kind of ringtone is that?*

"It's, ahh...." Disappointment mars his features as he pulls over to the side of the road. "I have to get this." He disappears out of the car, and my brows furrow as I watch him, his disappointment turning to anger until he jumps back in and his sadness hits me.

"Is it okay if I take you home?"

"Huh? Why? What happened?"

"Remember how I told you about my friend—the one that's constantly getting into trouble."

"I do..." I say slowly, my chest tight, filled with a mix of anger and concern. I'm all for friends helping friends, but sometimes I wonder if she's taking advantage of his kind nature.

"She needs help." *Of course she does.* "She's—"

"You don't have to explain. You're the one she needs, right?"

"I don't want to go." His puppy dog eyes plead with me to believe him, and my chest aches.

"It's fine. You're a good guy. I get it." I wink, biting back a smirk. "I'm in Sydney for a little while longer. Maybe I can meet you when you're done. I'll find a hotel close by and come back in a few—"

"Hotel? No way. You're staying at our place. No arguments. I'll make it up to you when I get back."

My nose scrunches. The thought of being stuck with Mason is not as thrilling as one would think, even with his enticingly ripped body and delicious smell. But when Jack smiles in anticipation, I can't say no.

"Okay. I'll be there."

"Thank you." He breathes a sigh of relief and some of my unease lessens. "I promise I won't be long."

D espite Jack giving me a key, I ring the doorbell and wait for Mason to open up. The sound of movement alerts me to his presence, and I swear I hear footsteps moving my way, but after two buzzes, he still hasn't answered the door. I'll bet my life savings that he saw me on the camera.

"Open up, Mason. I'm not going away."

The footsteps get louder again, and he fakes a smile as he yanks open the door. "Hey mate. Good to see you. What did you forget?"

"Nothing at all. I'm back to hang out with you. I'm staying for a few days. Yay!" I raise my hands to cheer and Mason's smile drops from his face, eliciting a triumphant grin on mine.

I'm about to sass him some more when he surprises me, his expression turning cold. "Where's Jack?"

"He had to do something and—"

"He had to *do* something? Did you two have a fight?"

"What? No. That friend of his that—"

"Are you fucking kidding me? He left you for Tracey?"

"I don't know her name, but he said she's always getting in trouble and—"

Mason growls, stopping me from saying more, and I find it oddly erotic. Which unfortunately adds to his appeal. My mind drifts to his wet body, the flex of his muscles when he— Shit. Nope. There are so many attractive people in Australia. I don't have to settle for an ass.

He curses under his breath, mumbling something about Jack being a dick before turning my way. "Are you okay?" His voice softens and it catches me off guard, making me giggle awkwardly.

"Of course. I'm fine. Why would you ask that?" I really *am* fine, despite the waver in my voice. I wasn't expecting him to care.

"Are you sure?"

"Yes," I say confidently. "I can take care of myself. I'm sure he won't be long. And if he is, I've got my car fifteen minutes away. I'm good."

"Good. She's not worth his time, but as I'm sure you've realized, Jack is much nicer than I am."

"Nooo. Really? I hadn't noticed."

With a shake of his head, Mason walks away, leaving me awkwardly standing in the entry. *What do I do now?*

I rock back on my heels for a beat until my stomach grumbles. Food. *Dammit.* Guess I'm helping myself.

After cursing the guys for not having any bacon or eggs lying around, I make a peanut butter sandwich, thankful I could at least find bread. I've just made myself comfortable on the couch when Mason appears.

His eyes flash to the sandwich raised to my mouth and he scowls. Whoops. *Am I not supposed to eat in here?*

"Is this—"

"I'm going to the beach." He cuts me off and I inhale sharply at his tone. Until it hits me...

"You're going to the beach?" I jump up, excitement coursing through me. "Can I come?"

"What?" His eyes grow comically large and I almost laugh, only holding back because I imagine that's the quickest way to piss him off. Instead, I smile. Politely.

"Can I come to the beach? *Please.*"

"Why?" He frowns and this time I have to physically bite back my amused response.

"To buy groceries," I deadpan, but he doesn't see the humor.

"The fuck?"

"To swim and sunbathe, Mason. Why is this concept so hard for you to grasp?"

"That's not what I meant. Why do you want to go with *me*?"

"Obviously because we get along so well."

He opens his mouth to argue, but my words must sink in because he hides a smile, shaking his head. "Ha. Ha."

"Can I come or not?" I plant my hands on my hips and huff, my brow raised.

"Sure, it's a free country." Boredom oozes from his tone. "I'm leaving in five minutes."

"Great. But I need fifteen. I'll meet you at the door."

I brush his shoulder as I walk past, and a spark of something runs through me. Ignoring what was obviously static electricity, I bounce up the stairs, a huge smile on my face. Jack may have promised the beach *later*, but I'm a water baby... I'll take the beach over anything else.

CHAPTER SEVEN
Mason

Between swimming and reading my book in the blistering sun, I manage to completely ignore Jenna's presence for the entire first hour of our "fun" outing. I'm proud to say, my eyes never once drifted her way while she sunbathed on her floral beach towel, her olive-green string bikini undone at the back, revealing a little too much side boob.

Nope, my gaze stayed firmly locked on my thriller.

Jenna disappears for a swim, and of course, I glance up at the exact moment she returns, water cascading down her bronzed skin, her wet hair slicked back off her face, and my stupid eyes bulge.

I'm surrounded by beautiful, half-naked women. All the time. Hell, when I'm at work, mixing cocktails and nodding along to the beats, I have women throwing themselves at me.

But there's something about Jenna Brooks that has me lowering my book so no one can see the semi in my board shorts.

I let my eyes linger for a beat, hiding behind my sunglasses. But when she fucking moans as she drops down to her towel, I quickly avert my gaze, silently cursing myself.

She's the devil. I'm sure of it.

Either that or I need to get laid.

"It's as if someone corralled the most attractive people in Australia and sent them here to welcome me. I've never seen so much beauty in one place." Jenna lifts her sunglasses as a young guy walks past, and I swear her eyes darken as she checks out his abs. "So many options." She sighs longingly and I scoff.

"Didn't you fly halfway around the world for my brother?"

"In a way, yes. But he's a friend."

"Does he know that?" I snap, finally drawing her gaze, my eyes flashing to my lap, relieved to find my bulge well and truly hidden.

The flash of a frown crosses her features, but before I can question it, it's gone. "I'm not sure." She shrugs. "I always thought so but then his last...never mind. I'm here because I wanted a break, and I figured it was time I paid your brother a visit. I skipped our Thanksgiving letter. The first one I've ever missed. Did he tell you that?"

Her eyes meet mine and my throat bobs as I nod, my heart pounding in my chest. "I knew, yes." *Please don't ask too many questions.*

"Well, I felt bad. So here I am." She smiles, lying back on her towel while stretching her body. Her back arches, and my gaze locks on her pert breasts falling out of the tiny triangles she's trying to pass off as bathers.

Swallowing a lump in my throat, I ignore the throbbing in my shorts as she continues.

"The funny thing is, I told him I was here to explain myself, but I've been avoiding the topic ever since. It's a long emotional story, and I'd rather keep things light between us. We only have a few days, a week at most. It's better to spend that time having fun."

My eyes flash to her face, scrutinising her expression. She says she wants to keep things light with Jack, and yet it almost feels like she's opening up to me.

The thought has my stomach twisting, but I don't question it.

Jenna lifts her sunglasses again, raising her perfectly manicured brows in question. "Does that make sense?"

"It does," I rush out. "But—"

"Goddddaaamn." She cuts me off, biting her lip as she moans, sitting up again. "An ass like that should be illegal. Please tell me you know her?"

"Her?" My eyes widen as my gaze darts to the woman she's staring at, and I instantly see the appeal, but... "You're attracted to women?" I glance back at Jenna, confused. I could have sworn she—

"I'm attracted to people," she clarifies, making me pause.

"What does that mean?"

"Gender doesn't matter."

"What matters?" My voice rises in pitch because I'm genuinely interested. I've never met anyone who likes both men and women. At least not on a personal level.

Jenna laughs, clearly amused, and I can't stop my frown from forming. *What did I say?*

"You look confused."

"I'd say curious."

"Okay. Curiosity is good."

"Good. Soooo..."

"Oh, right. Well for one, they need to have a good personality." She stares at me pointedly and I roll my eyes.

"Funny."

A smile lights up her face before she turns serious again. "In all honesty, it's usually a connection I feel."

I nod, pondering her words for a beat until my lips lift into a smile of my own. "I like that."

"Yeah?"

"Yeah. But I'm even more curious now. Does that mean you had a connection with her ass?"

Jenna laughs so hard, she snorts, falling back onto her towel, and my chest warms. She's never short of a comeback or sass, and she's constantly laughing. But there's something more real about her reaction just now. And though I shouldn't, I like that I elicited that happiness.

"Of course." She speaks between giggles. "A deep, *deep* connection. Look at her. I bet you felt it too."

"Oh, I already looked, and she is *fine.*"

"She's not the only one. Everyone here is *fine.*" She matches my intonation. "I'm jealous."

"Aren't you an actress in Hollywood? Don't try to pretend there aren't beautiful people over there."

"I'm not. They're just different."

I nod and reach for my water, suddenly thirstier than I've ever been in my life. Or maybe I need to distract myself so I don't think about Jenna hooking up with other beautiful women.

"Has your cock ever twitched over a hot piece of man?" she asks, and I choke on my drink, coughing to hide it. Not that it helps.

"Can you ever ask a question seriously?" I rasp, my throat croaky.

"Sorry." She giggles behind her hand. "Have you ever been attracted to a man?" She raises her brows as if to ask "is that better" and I stifle a smile.

"I haven't. I can appreciate a man being attractive, but my cock has never *twitched* as you say."

"So, you're not open to a threesome? Two men, one woman."

Jesus. Christ. I can't say I've ever considered it, but the idea is intriguing. If anything, it would be nice to rattle her with my response.

With my lip trapped between my teeth, I lean in closer, my face barely an inch from her ear. "Again... I can see the appeal. I'm sure there's something to be said about restraining yourself while you watch another man fuck the girl you want. Taking her after. But...it would depend."

Jenna's lips part, and I don't miss the way she squeezes her legs tighter together. "On what?"

"On who she was. If she was *my* girl...I wouldn't have to think about it. The answer would be a huge fuck no. I don't share. But a random hookup, maybe."

I shrug and her breath hitches as she spins in my direction, her nose brushing my cheek, forcing me to move back. "I like that," she whispers, her expression heated until she pulls herself out of it. "Good answer."

She's quiet for a beat until she pivots her entire body to face me and crosses her legs, her gaze now full of mischievous wonder. *What did I get myself into?* "How do you think your brother would react to that question?"

My brother. *Fuck.*

As if someone splashed cold water over me, I shiver, and any hint of an erection instantly disappears.

"Maybe you should ask him. I'm sure it classifies as '*keeping things light.*'" The hardness of my voice has Jenna's brows pinching, but before she can sass me, I jump up, needing some space.

"I'm going for a swim," I rush out, walking away, my chest tight with something I refuse to acknowledge.

She's here for my brother. For Jack. After his *last* letter.

And that means she's completely off-limits. At least she is to me.

J enna's ready to leave after my swim, and we walk back in uncomfortable silence. When we're home, I lead her through the yard to rinse and dry off, all while pretending she's someone else. Anyone else. Going as far as cutting her off when she tries to speak, mumbling something about a phone call I have to make.

A lie.

My muscles are tight as I take the stairs, two at a time, and the second I'm inside my room, I groan, proceeding to laugh at myself.

God, I'm a fucking idiot. It's Jenna. Jack's Jenna. Jack and Jenna. Their names don't even work together. But that's their problem, not mine.

It's time to fuck my hand, relieve some tension, and move on.

Who flies to another country after getting a dirty letter?

Jenna, apparently.

Grabbing a pair of shorts and a tee, I stalk past Jenna's room, praying she doesn't choose this moment to come upstairs. If she hasn't already.

I need to grab a new shampoo from the guest bathroom then I'll be on my way, back to the privacy of the master suite where I will remain until Jack gets home.

Which better be soon.

The image of him waltzing through the door without a care in the world has me wanting to knock some sense into him. He's beyond frustrating. I can't believe he left.

I'm once again angry on Jenna's behalf as I swing open the door, huffing to myself in the process, until...

"Jesus, fuck." I freeze, midstep. "What are you doing?" Jenna's in the shower, bent over, her phenomenal *naked* ass wriggling in the air, begging me to touch it.

She glances up at me from her compromising position and I groan, my cock instantly hardening.

"I'm shaving my legs." She shrugs.

"I can *see your ass*," I grate, my teeth clenched with the tension coursing through me.

"How else am I going to reach?"

"I don't know. Lift your leg and plant it against the wall."

"This is much more comfortable."

"That's nice but can you—"

"Why are you here, Mason?"

Shit. Fuck. "Sorry." She stands and spins slightly, forcing me to look away to avoid full frontal nudity. Seeing her in her bathers was hard enough, seeing her bare ass was harder still, but seeing her pussy...that's not something I can come back from. "I'm leaving."

I grab the door but pause at the threshold. *Dammit.* "I need shampoo." I walk backward, blindly reaching for the drawer under the sink, and of course she fucking giggles.

My hand curls around the shampoo and I remember she's a girl. Obviously, but... "There's better body wash here." I reach around and lift up the bottle. "It's for women. Jack uses whatever is in front of him, not wanting to overload his head with too many decisions in the morning, so I moved it out."

"That's kind of you, though I don't mind smelling like a man. Is this what you use?" She moves, presumably to grab the body wash from the shower floor, but I don't dare look. Instead, my muscles twitch. *Why is that so fucking hot?*

"Which one have you got?" I ask, clenching my teeth once more.

"Have a look?"

Dammit, Jenna.

"It doesn't matter. Use what you like."

"What's wrong? Never seen a naked woman before?"

What the fuck? She's challenging me now?

Growing some balls, I raise an eyebrow and spin confidently, but the second I see her, I falter.

She's fucking breathtaking.

There is no other way to describe her.

And from the sass in her expression, she knows it.

"This one?" She holds up the bottle with one hand and bites a nail on the other. While I couldn't tell you what she's holding if my life depended on it.

The bottle is positioned next to her pebbled nipples, and it's taking all my power not to join her in the shower, eager to twist one.

My throat dries as I stare at her, my gaze lowering to her bare pussy, imagining what it would be like to run my tongue through her heat, to lap up her—

"Mase." She moans my name, her tone as desperate as I feel. It's barely louder than a whisper but it pulls me out of my lust.

What the fuck am I doing?

A door slams downstairs and I curse as I jump, my heart pounding so hard it hurts.

"I'm home," Jack calls out and I curse louder.

"Use the men's," I growl, dumping the floral-smelling shit back in the drawer, my body vibrating with unease as I hightail it out of there.

Why the hell didn't I leave?

But more than that, *why does it feel like that's the least of my worries?*

CHAPTER EIGHT
Jenna

I stare at the bathroom door, shocked at Mason's sudden departure. But when I get downstairs after I'm dressed and find him and Jack in the kitchen, it all makes sense.

Jack's home, and we wouldn't want him to find us like that now, would we? *Why do I sound bitter?* I'm clearly out of sorts.

I'd turned in the shower to mess with Mason. I love my body. I've never been afraid to flaunt it. It was supposed to be a fun way to tease him. But the joke was on me. Because no one has ever looked at me the way he did. The fire in his eyes lit a spark inside me and, arousal aside, he made me feel desired unlike any other. *I don't know how to describe it.* I felt it from my chest, right down to my toes. My entire body came to life.

From one look. One fervent gaze.

On top of that, there was his reaction to me liking both men and women. Most guys I tell stare at me in disbelief, or smirk, asking for a threesome. But Mason's inquisitive gaze gave me a buzz. And his response. "I like it." *My God.* He's a whole different species from his brother. I told Jack I thought one of his friends was beautiful last night by the pool, and he laughed as though I was joking, changing the subject.

It wasn't a negative response, per se, but he didn't consider it long enough to ask questions. I like that Mason did.

But he's Mason.

I shouldn't be thinking about him like that. *Like nothing.* I'm not thinking about him like anything.

Jack announces our dinner has arrived, telling me he hopes I'm happy with pizza. And of course, I am. *Who doesn't love pizza?*

He sets up the food on the dining room table, and when I take my seat opposite Mason, I suppress a laugh. "Is that pasta?"

He glances down at his bowl. "Ah, yep." He eyes my pizza, his face contorting. *Guess that answers my question.* I snort to myself.

Jack sits down, and an uncomfortable tension hovers around the table as we eat. Though, I'm ninety percent sure I'm the only one that feels it. I'm more convinced when Jack casually asks Mason about his day, a brotherly smile on his face.

"I forgot to ask, how were the waves this morning? Kai said they're up and down this week. I don't want to wake up early if they're not worth it."

A tingle shoots through me. Mason surfs? *Why does that make him at least twenty percent hotter?* I picture him gliding across the waves while Jack mentions something about his board, and I almost choke on my food. Jack said he surfs too and yet... my mind did not go there.

I feel nothing.

Which is a good thing, right? It's the best thing for our friendship. I need to push his letter out of my mind. He hasn't mentioned it at all, and he hasn't made a move. This is the best possible outcome. I'm not attracted to him. He's not attracted to me. It's perfect.

I can relax and enjoy myself without the pressure of what's to come. I could even find an Aussie to hook up with without feeling guilty.

Mason growls and my heart jolts as my eyes flash to his. *Is he reading my mind?*

I smile when I find him looking at Jack, until I realize they're in some kind of standoff. *What the hell did I miss?*

"Can we talk about this later?" Jack subtly nods my way, and Mason's eyes dart to mine.

"Yep. Later." His chair scrapes on the floor as he jumps up, stalking from the room and Jack smiles my way.

"Sorry about that. Big brothers, hey." He shrugs as longing tugs at my middle. *He has no idea how lucky he is.*

Jack heads off for a shower after dinner and I take that as my cue to head to my room.

My eyes drift to the bathroom as I walk past and I almost wish Mason had given me the floral body wash, so I could find out if he's right. If Jack would use it without thought. I smile, imagining Jack smelling like roses.

Though, it could have been Mason's way of delaying his departure. And something about that excites me even more. He's been grumpy for a majority of the two days I've known him, but I've seen glimpses of something else, something real. It's obvious his asshole persona is a front. A mask to hide behind.

And I'm dying to know *why*.

Grabbing my book, I jump into bed, preparing for a quiet night. It may only be eight, but you'd think I'd been awake for days with how tired I feel.

I'm halfway through the first page when my phone buzzes and Blair's name pops up on my screen.

Speaking of being awake, it's two a.m. there.

Blair: How's Australia? We haven't heard from you since your "he's not a psycho" text. And while I'm grateful you confirmed that, I need details. You're usually the queen of details

And she usually avoids them. She must miss me.

Me: Why are you awake?

Blair: I was worried

My chest warms and a smile pulls at my lips. If soulmates exist, I've already found mine in Blair. She's my polar opposite, and yet, I couldn't imagine life without her. It's nice having someone who cares.

Me: Australia is wonderful. I think I might move here

I'm joking, but I'm not going to pretend the thought hasn't crossed my mind.

Blair: What? For real?

Me: No. But I want all the hotness to come with me when I go home

Blair: Hotness, huh? How's Jack?

Me: He's adorable and sweet and fun

Hayley: Uh-oh

Jeez, Hayley's awake too?

Blair: What's uh-oh? What did I miss?

Hayley: He's adorable and sweet. Both great qualities... What's missing is what she didn't say

I smile at Hayley's message. She gets me too. Sometimes more than Blair does. Maybe I have *two* soulmates. Soulmates can be friends, right?

Speaking of friends...

Me: I think we're destined to remain platonic and I'm okay with that

Blair: You are? Was he not the man his letter suggested? All talk?

Me: Nothing's happened between us

Hayley: Did you talk about it?

Me: Nope. It hasn't felt right

My mind drifts back to the fire in Mason's eyes when he saw me naked. If it was him I was friends with, instead of Jack, I would have mentioned it. Demanded he tell me what the hell it all meant. I can't explain why it's different for the two of them. It's just a feeling I get.

Blair: Does that mean you're coming home?

I type out a message mentioning Mason but think better of it. I wouldn't know what to say. I don't understand it myself.

All I know is that I'm not ready to leave. Not yet.

Me: I'm going to stay for a few more days and take a Christmas Day flight home

Blair: Christmas Day! No. Can't you come on Christmas Eve? You can spend Christmas with us

Me: Thanks, but I'm okay. I'll come to San Francisco and annoy you both when you're home next week

Blair: You better

Hayley: Can't wait

Blair: I'm sorry Jack wasn't your soulmate

I laugh out loud, pulling the comforter over my head.

Me: I'm not

A soft knock penetrates my hiding place, and I sit up to listen out for it again. "Jenna, it's me."

Jack.

Disappointment runs through me, but I cough as though that'll fix it, refusing to acknowledge what it means. "Come in."

Jack opens the door and smiles when he finds me in bed. "If you're not jet-lagged, I'm going to make popcorn and watch a movie. Want to join me?"

"I'd love to. I'll be down in a minute."

"Great." His smile widens and yep...it's adorable. He has golden retriever energy but doesn't come across as loyal and caring as that. After exchanging letters for eight years, I'm still trying to work him out.

By the time I drag myself out of bed and make it downstairs, Jack has *Love Actually* paused on the opening airport scene, and my stomach knots. I'm really not feeling Christmas this year, and while it's not something I can easily ignore, I wasn't expecting to be constantly hit in the face with it. The beach was perfect. There were no signs of Christmas. Just an open space full of gorgeous people.

"Christmas, huh?" I force a happiness I don't feel, and Jack instantly believes it.

"Hell, yeah. Gotta get into the spirit."

"What about *Die Hard*?" *That I can do.*

"*Die Hard*? That's not a Christmas movie."

"What?" My jaw drops as my question echoes from behind me.

"Sometimes I worry about you, bro." Mason's deep voice filters through the air, and my head involuntarily twists toward the sound. "*Die Hard* is definitely a Christmas movie," he agrees with me.

"Maybe." Jack shrugs, clearly still annoyed at Mason from whatever was said earlier.

"So..."

"I'm not feeling it." He shrugs again.

Mason opens his mouth to speak but I cut in. "What about something different then? Something non-Christmassy."

"Something non-Christmassy at Christmas time?"

"Yep."

Jack frowns in confusion, and I'd laugh if I wasn't about to give in and watch *Love Actually*. "It's—"

"Two against one, little bro. We're watching *Die Hard*." Mason jumps over the arm of the couch opposite us and lands on the cushion, making himself comfortable.

"I thought you were going out?" Jack snaps, his gaze briefly flashing my way as his eyes widen toward his brother. If he's trying to signal something to Mason, he doesn't get it, because he simply shrugs, pointing to the TV.

"My plans changed and I want some Bruce Willis."

Without another word, Jack goes back to their movie home page and sure enough, *Die Hard* is listed under Christmas movies. He scoffs as he presses play, but I don't watch the screen. Instead, my curious gaze lands on Mason. *Was that for me? Or did he do it to piss off his brother?* He's not even watching; he's got his face buried in his phone.

A few seconds pass and I'm about to force myself to pay attention when his head lifts and our eyes lock. He shoots me a wink, and my breath catches as he turns to face the TV, the smallest of smiles playing on his lips.

He did it for me. And I'm not sure I like how good that makes me feel.

CHAPTER NINE
Mason

O f course being nice would come back and bite me in the ass. I should have walked away thirty minutes ago, but my stupid ego forced me to see it through. To pretend I'm enjoying the movie I desperately wanted to watch, acting as though I'm completely oblivious to the giggles and flirting coming from the opposite couch.

The movie ends and I jump up so fast you'd think the couch was on fire. But it's not fast enough.

Jack pulls Jenna to her feet, laughing richly as he whispers in her ear.

"I've been drooling over it since I first arrived," she tells him, her eyes wide with excitement.

"Let's do it."

"Gah. Yes!"

Gah? I didn't take Jenna as a "gah" type of girl, but what do I know? And what the fuck has she been drooling about?

The letter comes to mind and my stomach sinks. Not that I get time to process it before Jack's phone erupts in a siren and the room stills. Me included. Jack curses while Jenna steps back, her subtle eye roll making it clear she knows what that particular ringtone means.

Though, I doubt she has anything to worry about this time. Not with the way tonight's playing out. If Jack wants Jenna, now's his chance. Even he's smart enough not to walk away from that.

"I'll be back," he says, surprising me, my eyes flashing to Jenna's to find her expression neutral.

"Sure thing. I'll get my bikini on and meet you by the pool upstairs."

Jack leaves the room and I groan under my breath. *Mother. Fucker.* The pool on our balcony runs right past my bedroom window. I should have gone out. Why the hell did I cancel—

"What's that about?" Jenna asks, cutting into my thoughts, her eyebrows perfectly arched.

"What about?" I expect her to ask about Jack, but I'm off base.

"The groan." She playfully smirks.

"Oh, nothing important," I lie. "I'm shocked you're bothering with a bikini. You're not shy about your body. It's dark; why not skinny-dip?" I'm trying to be an ass except now I'm picturing her naked in my pool and that's not ideal.

Jenna's head drops back as she laughs out loud. "You'd love that, wouldn't you? Maybe you could join us. I believe I'm owed a peep show."

"As tempting as that sounds..." I fake a smile, letting the sarcasm drip from my tone. "I'm good. You kids have fun."

Jenna grins but I don't let her say anything else as I turn, walking away quicker than I need to, her parting giggle sending a shiver down my spine. *Why am I letting her get under my skin?* I promised myself I wouldn't.

I pass Jack as I walk into the hall, and the regret in his eyes stops me in my tracks. *Nooo. Fuck. Surely not.* Come on, Jack, you're better than that.

Taking a deep breath, I spin around at the same moment he delivers the blow to Jenna. "I have to go. I won't be as long this time but—"

"No," I boom from behind him, making him jump. "For once in your life, think about what you're doing."

"I am." He looks back at me, a scowl marring his expression. "Tracey needs me. She's—"

"Using you, Jack. Can't you see that?"

"She doesn't have anyone else, asshole. Just because you're not capable of caring about others doesn't mean I have to be selfish."

Jenna gasps as her gaze bounces between us. "I don't think—"

"It's fine," I cut her off. "You're right. I'm the selfish one. Go." *What do I know about being there for someone who can't look after themselves?*

With a glare my way, Jack steps closer to Jenna and whispers softly so I can't hear what he's saying. She smiles back at him before he turns to leave.

My jaw aches from how tightly I'm clenching my teeth, but it stops me from saying more as he stalks toward the garage. *What the hell is he thinking?*

He flips me off, slamming the door, and I lose my restraint. "Real mature, dickhead."

I huff as I turn around, finding Jenna's curious gaze locked on mine. "You didn't have to do that. He's free to do as he pleases."

"I love him but he's a fucking idiot. All he ever does is *do what he pleases.*"

She laughs and the lightness of it instantly calms me. She's clearly not as affected by this as I am. But she has no idea how fucked up that relationship is. She calls, and he goes running. I used to think he had a crush on her, and that he was waiting for his shot. I've since discovered he likes being her hero. It gives him some kind of fucked-up high, which was fine when it wasn't affecting anyone else, but now, he's ditching Jenna for her.

"How many years are there between you and Jack?" Jenna's voice cuts into my anger, her curious gaze returning.

"Six," I bark before huffing in apology. "I'm thirty-three," I say, softer this time.

"And still living with your brother?" She raises an eyebrow, biting back a smile, and I hate that it makes me chuckle. Her teasing should piss me off. She doesn't know me. But...

"Unfortunately, yes."

"Why don't you move out?" *Well, Jenna, I ask myself that question on a daily basis.*

"Would you?" I counter, waving my hand around the space. I love this house, but it's much more complicated than that.

"Definitely not." Jenna snorts, her expression awed. "This house is incredible. I'd kick my brother out. If I had one."

There's a sadness to her tone that has my smile fading. "Are you an only child?" I ask, wanting to keep her talking.

"I am. I would have loved to have a sibling growing up. However, I can also see the challenges."

"Having a younger brother who treats houseguests like shit?" I smile until Jenna shakes her head.

"No. The responsibility for said younger brother."

"What?" A pounding raps at my rib cage, the beat getting stronger the longer Jenna stares at me, seeing me better than anyone ever has. And she barely knows me. *What do I say to that?*

"Do you ever get the chance to let loose?" She breaks my inner spiral, and whether she sees how uncomfortable I am or doesn't want the conversation to get too deep, I appreciate the change of subject.

"Of course," I lie.

"You nursed the same beer for seven hours at the pool party yesterday."

"I had two beers, thank you." I smirk and she lets out a snort laugh. "Not everyone has to drink to let loose. I have my ways." My voice deepens of its own accord, making my admission sound much dirtier than it is.

Jenna's eyes fill with intrigue and I almost laugh, guessing where her mind went.

"Like what?" she asks.

"The waves." I shrug nonchalantly and her lips twist.

"Wrong answer."

"Wrong answer?"

"Yep." She pops the *p*. "That doesn't count. Let's go."

"Where are we going?"

"You're going to meet me at the pool. We're doing shots."

"Shots?" I stare, unimpressed. That sounds like hell, and something my brother would do. I see the effects of shots whenever I'm at work.

"You're going to love it. I'll tell you what... For every shot you have, you can ask me a personal question."

Her reaction to Christmas comes to mind, and my intrigue gets the better of me. "Fine."

"Yes! I'll be back in five minutes." She rushes off, but the excitement in her eyes lingers in my mind. It would be much easier if I wasn't goddamn attracted to her. Too late for that.

Five minutes later, I'm in the pool waiting, but when fifteen minutes tick by, I question my sanity. *Is she playing me?*

Palms flat on the pool's edge, I lift my body out of the water and freeze, my muscles locked as Jenna walks outside.

My throat tightens at the sight of her. She's the embodiment of a goddess, her gold bikini sparkling in the light, her soft curls cascading down her front, covering her chest. The innocence of it makes her all the more alluring and I can't drag my eyes away, desperate to see what's underneath.

"Oh, yay, you got the good stuff." Her words jolt me as she points to a bottle of vodka beside me, and I find a smile gracing her lips when I finally look at her face.

Her gaze drops until she openly ogles my chest, and the fire in her eyes forces me back into the pool.

"If you're making me do shots, I want it to taste good. This one's flavoured." I shrug because I'm not sure that makes it much better, but it's worth a try.

"Flavored?" Jenna snaps out of her leering and rushes over, grabbing the bottle in her grasp. "Vanilla?" Her smile widens. "This is going to be fun."

I smile back at her, but the pit in my stomach tells me I'm not as sure as she is.

But God, I hope she's right.

My mind spins as I stare unfocused into Jenna's dark eyes, the reflection of the moon illuminating her features. I blink a few times as I replay what she said.

I've had my heart trapped in my throat for the past two shots, and I'm not sure I can take it anymore.

The first few questions were tame, with the two of us throwing around easy topics like our first kiss or when we lost our virginity. But the last couple have been a little more personal—do I consider Jack and me to be friends? And have we ever liked the same girl?

Both of which were yes.

Jenna keeps her expression schooled while I think, yet there's a glint in her eyes as she passes me a shot glass, the vodka spilling over the edge. "Your turn."

I nod and tilt my head back, closing my eyes as the cool liquid burns my throat. I have no idea what my limit is when it comes to shots. I haven't done anything like this since university. However, I'm not about to back down. I can't.

When I'm finished drinking, I lower the glass slowly, opening my eyes to find her lust-filled gaze staring back. *And fuck me.*

If she keeps looking at me like that, I'm... No, I'm not going to do anything. No matter how badly I want to.

Before I can speak, her eyes drop to my mouth and she bites her lip, tugging the flesh between her teeth.

God. She's been sent here to tempt me. My own personal siren. "Why don't you like Christmas?" I blurt, instantly bringing her out of her daze.

"What?" She blinks a few times.

"Why don't you like Christmas?" I repeat and my chest burns with regret. Talk about jumping from zero to one hundred.

"Let's call it abandonment issues." Jenna's eyes narrow and she rips the shot glass from my hand, knocking back two shots in quick succession. I move to apologise until she swipes her thumb across her lip, rendering me speechless as she sucks it into her mouth.

"What were you and Jack arguing about at dinner?" she retorts, her eyes harsher than they were a few seconds ago.

"You," I answer without thought, my brain malfunctioning.

"What? Why?" She frowns but her questions make me smile.

"Uh-uh." I waggle my finger. "It's my turn." *And I'd rather not get into that right now.*

"Fine. Ask away."

I gulp down another shot, ignoring the dull ache behind my eyes. "Why'd you come to Australia?" I ask, catching myself off guard.

Jenna shrugs but answers without missing a beat. "Your brother."

"Why?"

Dammit. I wait for the grin and she delivers, right on cue. "Uh-uh. My turn." She raises the bottle to her mouth, taking a swig, not bothering to use the glass anymore.

"Have you ever had a serious relationship?" she asks, her intense stare penetrating mine.

"No." I'm quick to respond. "Have you?"

"No. When was the last time you had sex?"

"A few weeks ago. You?"

"The night before I came here."

I internally cringe but wave for her to continue, and the rapid-fire questions begin, the alcohol seemingly forgotten.

"Have you ever been arrested?"

"Have you ever smoked weed?

"Done drugs?"

"Hurt someone?"

We go back and forth, barely a breath taken between us, until I ask a question I instantly regret. "Have you ever kissed Jack?" *Fuck. Why the hell would I ask that?*

Jenna hisses as she pauses, grabbing the vodka again, taking another a sip, answering without emotion. "No."

"You *paused*," I rasp and *Jesus. Stop. Questioning. Her.*

Unperturbed, Jenna smiles. "I did. I was curious."

"About what?"

The water sloshes as she moves closer and my breath catches. She jokes about Australia having the most beautiful people in the world, but I have never seen anyone more perfect than her. Especially now with her flushed cheeks and the spark in her eye.

A spark that should probably make me nervous.

She stops in front of me, her smile flirtatious as she bites her lip again, and nothing could stop my gaze from dropping to her mouth.

"Do you want to kiss me?" she whispers, her honey voice fucking with my head, exactly like the siren I believe her to be. "Or do you need mistletoe for that?"

"No to both," I scoff, moving closer, the lie tasting bitter on my tongue, my entire body tingling with need.

"Good." She stares defiantly, her chest rising with shallow breaths, her eyes bouncing between mine, and I have no doubt her next words are going to be a lie.

"I don't want to kiss you either."

CHAPTER TEN
Mason

O ur surroundings fade away until all I can see is Jenna, the rise and fall of her chest, her deep brown gaze penetrating mine, her lips parted. My breath catches. She's captivating and I can't look away. I can't be the first to break our stare.

Water ripples as she shifts, bringing her closer. It's so subtle that if I wasn't hyperaware of her every move, I may not have noticed it. Tension wraps around us like a suffocating hug, and as though feeling it, Jenna shivers, forcing me to bite back a groan.

The energy cracks between us, and my entire body tingles as I watch her. Locked under her spell. "Jen—"

Her foot touches my leg and I jolt, a pain shooting through my elbow as I knock the edge of the pool, hitting the shot glass as I do. It drops into the water, and I watch it sink beneath the surface, my restraint following after, my resolve drowning in the darkness. "Fuck it."

Jenna gasps as I close the distance between us, cupping her face and slamming my mouth to hers. She freezes for a beat before grabbing my waist, her moves desperate as she pulls me closer, our bodies flush, her lips pressed to mine.

Releasing her face, I grip under her ass and lift her in my arms, groaning when she wraps her legs around me, her arms circling my neck.

My lips part and she swipes her tongue between them, the taste of vanilla combined with *her* flooding my mouth. Our tongues clash with an explorative force and I'm lost in her touch. But when she quivers against me, I freeze, slowing my movements until a sigh escapes her.

The change in pace brings a tenderness to the kiss that sends a ripple through my chest, and I struggle to ignore the tightness that follows.

Curling my hand into her hair, I tug on the strands and she hisses under her breath, her fervour increasing, bringing us back to the tempo I need.

She twists in my arms, her back arching, her centre rubbing along my length, and I vibrate with need. My blood pools south, my skin burning everywhere she touches.

I'm losing my goddamn mind and I want more.

Testing the waters, I rock my hips, grinding my cock against her pussy, my palm twitching under her ass, itching to push her bikini to the side. Just an inch. Enough to sink my fingers inside her. To feel her walls sucking me in.

My length throbs, and Jenna moans against my mouth. "Do it," she whispers. "I need you to touch me."

"Fuuck," I grunt from the back of my throat, adding "mind reader" to the list of her dangerous traits.

Spinning her around, I hold her against the edge and cup her neck, angling her face to deepen the kiss, sucking her lip until she whimpers softly. "*Please.*"

She squirms with need as I kiss a path across her cheek, nibbling my way down her throat, sucking her flesh as my palm settles between her legs.

A rushed breath escapes her and her head falls back, her breasts lifting above the water. When her nipples pebble from the fresh night air, I flatten my tongue over a bud, loving when her body shakes.

She's fucking beautiful in this moment—in all the fucking moments—and I'm screwed.

Curling my finger against her bikini bottom, I tease her pussy as I nibble on her breast, and she cries out in need, releasing her hold on me.

I'm about to change position when she grabs my cock over my shorts, wrapping her fingers around my length, her eyes locked on mine. "Fuck, you're big."

"*Jesus. Christ.*" I buck against her hand, my balls tightening from her touch. A single touch. "God, that feels good. *You* feel incredible."

She wriggles around, her lips meeting my ear as she bites my lobe, whispering the words I need more than anything else. "I want it all."

Fuuuck. I want that too.

My ringtone blares from the deck beside us, the shrill sound ripping me out of the moment. I rear back at the same time Jenna pulls away, her breathing ragged, her eyes darting to my phone.

And my mind goes to Jack.

A guttural groan flies from my chest, and my heart pounds with a force I can't control. "What the fuck are we doing? You're Jack's. He's—"

"Excuse me." Jenna recoils into the wall behind her, hitting me with an expression full of rage. "I'm no one's goddamn property, least of all Jack's."

I cringe. Least of all *mine*. "That's not what I meant, and you know it."

"Actually, I don't. You're going to have to *spell* it out."

"Why are you here, Jenna?" I grate, my rage now mimicking hers. "Why'd you fly halfway around the world to see him?"

Jenna sucks in a breath, her eyes wide as she quips back, "That's none of your goddamn business."

"You made it my business when you..." I trail off because she didn't do anything. It was all me. I'm the one that made a move. I'm the one that can't keep my eyes off her, my hands off her. She may have tempted me, but I'm the one that lost control.

I've never been that guy. Only I can't seem to stay the fuck away from her.

She's off-limits. Whether she knows it or not.

"What the hell did I do to make it your business? I—"

"Sorry," I interrupt, reaching out then thinking better of it, letting my hand drop with a splash between us. "I didn't mean that either, but this can't happen. It *shouldn't* have happened."

With Jenna's back to the light, the halo effect makes it hard to see her features, but it's easy to sense she's about to argue. "Jenna, I—"

"It's okay." She sighs, the edge to her voice softening. "It was just a kiss. No big deal."

A sour taste fills the back of my throat but I nod through it. "Just a kiss."

"Glad we agree." She smiles but it's no more real than the lie that just passed through my lips, and I hate that it's better this way.

Without another word, she swims toward the ladder and curls her hands around the bar, shaking as she climbs out of the pool. I watch her, unmoving, my stomach knotted with regret.

"I'm going to bed." She grabs her towel from the lounge chair, her tone void of emotion as she stands tall.

My phone rings again and Jenna stares down at it as she walks past, letting droplets of water fall to the screen. "It's not even him." She scoffs, and I swear her lip curls in disgust as she turns toward the door. "It's Becca."

Fuck. My eyes slam shut as I flinch. "That's not—"

"I don't care."

"I care," I call out after her, pulling myself out of the water, knocking the vodka over, ignoring the remnants as it spills onto the deck. "She's a friend. It's a joke."

"Doesn't matter." Jenna waves me off like it's nothing, though I'm not stupid; I already know her better than that.

"Jenna—"

"Fuck off."

Yep. She's pissed. But I goddamn deserve it.

Of all the fucking people who could be calling me right now, it had to be Becca. She set her photo as a close-up of her chest, her tits practically spilling out of her bikini. Joking that it might prompt me to think about sex every once in a while. Hoping I'd go and get laid. Apparently, I'm an irritable motherfucker when I'm abstaining. Not that I do it on purpose. I don't prioritize my sex life. My hand works fine and sex has never been memorable for me. It's always just been a need.

In this case, the joke is on Becca because her photo fucking backfired. If she hadn't called, I'd be having sex right now. I *wanted it.*

Gotta love friends.

Despite being summer, the chill of the night air follows me inside, and I've just made it to the landing when Jenna's door slams down the hall, making me shiver for a different reason. I throw my head back and groan, not bothering to hide the sound as frustration consumes me.

What the fuck is wrong with me?

I can't decide what's more messed up...the fact that I kissed her or the fact that I pulled away.

I'm not usually a big drinker, but with the vodka no longer disrupting my brain, I have too much sense to think. And I don't need that right now.

A quick change and a phone call later, I'm running downstairs to meet Kai, jumping in his car to head God knows where, but immediately feeling better.

Because at the very least, now I can breathe.

A soft pounding rouses me ahead of my alarm, and it's not until I sit up that I realize it's my head. *Fucking Kai.* My groan rumbles in the back of my throat, and I cough as even that pains me.

Give the guy an inch and he'll take a fucking mile. Or in Kai's case, tell him I want to drink and he gets me fucking plastered.

After checking the time, I drop back to the pillow and smile, sinking deep into the cloudy comfort. I could stay here all day. If it wasn't the *one* day a year that I actually set a morning alarm.

Speaking of...it feels like no time has passed when it blares in my ear and I groan again, forcing myself to get up.

Hitting go on my latest playlist, an image of Jenna plays on my mind. It hasn't left since she walked away. Her taste still lingers on my tongue. No matter how hard I try, I can't shake her.

When I'm done getting ready, I pull up my messages to Kai and type random letters, distracting myself as I walk past Jenna's door.

At the last second, I fail, glancing up to find her door open, and I falter. With her bed made, the vacant room has my stomach sinking. *Did she leave?* My eyes bounce to Jack's room to find it equally bare, and a burning sensation wells in my chest. *Are they together?*

Were their doors open when I got home? Were—

Fuck. What am I doing?

Cursing myself, I shake off my thoughts and jog down the stairs, until hushed voices from the TV pull me up short.

Jenna's sprawled on the couch like she owns the place, and a relieved smile graces my lips, *until* I remember it shouldn't.

It would be significantly easier to ignore her if I didn't find her goddamn intoxicating.

She moans and it's anything but sexual, yet I'm taken back to her dripping body pressed against mine, her quiet mewls as I was grinding into her.

"Why the hell is it so freaking hard to find something to watch over here?" Jenna mumbles under her breath, loud enough to pull me back to the present. I follow her gaze to the TV, and it only takes a few flashes of red and green to know why she's complaining.

And the urge to heal her takes over me.

Without thinking, I stalk over and grab the remote from her hand, switching the TV off and tossing the remote out of her reach.

"What'd you do that for?" She gapes, her expression morphing from confusion to anger right before my eyes.

"Two reasons." I hold up two fingers, and she scoffs. "One, you're flicking through network television, not our streaming services, and you're never going to find anything good. Two, we're going out."

"Who?"

"You. And. Me." I point a finger her way then direct it back to my chest, opting for the asshole approach over something more sincere. She's not the type to go for the latter. Not yet, anyway.

Jenna laughs manically, her expression wild as she crosses her arms over her chest. "Yeah, that's not going to happen."

"Why? Are you pissed off at me? I thought you didn't care."

Fury mars her features and I almost give in, but I can't deny that I like pushing her buttons, especially when it leads to a spark of fire igniting in her eyes. "What do you want, Mason?"

"I've got a job to do and you're coming with me."

"Why would I do that? I'm *Jack's*." His name seductively rolls off her tongue, and I physically wince, unable to hide it.

Jenna smirks triumphantly, but her verbal dig tells me that I've got her and I can't stop a little sneer of my own.

"Jack's not here, is he?" I take a guess that I'm right, since he's spent the last eight years avoiding this day, and even if he didn't, he's never up this early. "On top of that, you're in a country you've never been to and instead of exploring, you're watching TV."

"It's barely nine. I've got most of the day."

"So, you have a better offer?" I stare at her in challenge, refusing to give in now that I'm close, an idea coming to mind.

She stands and juts a hip, clearly hoping her defiant stance will sway me to let it go. Instead, I almost laugh because she's not going to win. I can be a stubborn motherfucker when I want to be. And at this moment, I've never wanted anything more.

"We're going." I spin on the spot, walking back into the hall. "Come on. We can't be late."

"I'm not—"

'You're coming. Hurry up."

Jenna huffs adorably, and I bite back a smile as I continue on my way, only pausing when she calls out.

"Can you at least tell me if I need to change?" I turn to face her, my eyes raking over her body, slowly drinking her in. Not that I need to. I noticed what she was wearing the second I walked in the room, and I hate to admit, she looks damn good in everything.

Today she's wearing ripped black jeans and a Guns N' Roses band tee knotted at the front, showing off a sliver of her alluring skin.

The outfit's perfect for what I have planned, but she doesn't need to know that.

"You're good," I tell her instead, my voice neutral, hiding the fact that I'm still thinking about the way her skin sizzled under my touch.

"Oh-kay. Thanks. But is it appropriate?"

"Mostly." I shrug.

"Mostly? What the hell does that mean?" She frowns and I stifle a laugh.

"Get your ass outside. I'll meet you in a minute."

Her angry gaze burns a hole in the back of my head and I internally cringe. There's a good chance she might hate me for this, though something tells me she won't. And if it changes her mood toward Christmas, I'm willing to take that risk.

CHAPTER ELEVEN
Jenna

As I walk out into the front yard, the roar of an engine pulls my focus to the closed garage door. *Is that a motorcycle? God, please let it be a motorcycle.*

Anticipation coils in my stomach as the door lifts and a thick black tire comes into view. But it's not until I see the most beautiful Harley-Davidson that my panties all but melt away. I bite back a giddy squeal, my lips parting with desire.

Damn him for making himself a whole lot sexier. As if it wasn't hard enough to be pissed at him already.

It takes a lot to hurt me when it comes to casual sex, and last night was no exception. It was an utter lapse in judgment. On both our parts. I'd love to blame Mason, only I can't. While I may not have any romantic feelings for Jack, and I'm ninety percent sure he doesn't feel anything for me, I still shouldn't be messing with his brother. Because what if I'm ninety percent wrong?

I didn't come here to hurt Jack. In fact, I'm beginning to wonder what the hell I'm doing here at all...and I can't hate Mason for that. No matter how badly I want to.

God knows he's given me plenty of reasons. If I were anyone else, I'm sure I'd be bitter over his brutal rejection. Yet, all I could do was laugh, because to a degree it all makes sense. He doesn't want to hurt his brother any more than I do, and the girl blowing up his phone... Somehow, I knew, without confirmation from the panic in his eyes, that it wasn't what it looked like.

It's barely been two days, and yet, I know without a doubt that Mason's not the booty-call type. I only *acted* pissed off to fuck with him a little.

It's what I do.

And apparently, it's what Mason does too because...of course he rides a motorcycle.

As though he hasn't noticed my staring, he walks the bike forward and stops beside me, only acknowledging my existence after jumping off and offering me a helmet. "Ground rules," he snaps, as if he has *any* right to be mad at me after the shit he pulled last night. Instead of arguing, I let this play out. "No talking to me while I'm riding. No screaming in my ear. No complaining about the wind."

He waves the helmet and I snatch it from his hand. "What if I don't want to get on your death trap?"

"You do."

"I do?"

"Jenna, you were practically drooling at the sight of it. I bet you'd beg me for a ride if I said you couldn't come. Hell, if I checked, I'm certain I'd find your panties soaked from how much you want this."

Heat pools at my center and I hate that he's not wrong. "You'll never know. You blew your shot last night."

"Good. I got more than enough after one kiss and the peep show you gave me."

"Use that image a lot, do you?"

"What?" His brows furrow until he seemingly gets my joke and a smile tugs at his lips. "Twice already, so thanks for adding to my spank bank."

"You're welcome." I grin widely as a warmth runs through me, the visual assaulting my mind. *God-fucking-dammit.* That shouldn't be so hot.

"Back to the bike," I say, matching his bitterness. "If I agree to your stupid rules, can we go already?"

"Yep." He grabs my bag from the ground beside my feet and I study his movement, only then taking in what he's wearing. And hell... He's trying to kill me. The asshole rejected me and now he's walking around like sex on legs.

To undoubtedly fuck with my head, he's wearing tight black jeans and a weathered leather jacket. I've never seen anything sexier. The jacket's open, giving me a glimpse of his fitted white tee, and I almost drool for real.

Why does he have to be so damn appealing?

"Are you coming?" He raises an eyebrow, biting back another cocky grin.

"Yep. I was born ready for this."

"Okay." He turns away, curling his leg over the seat, securing himself in position, then pats the space behind him. "Final rule. Don't let go."

Before I have the chance to respond, he covers his face with the visor and grabs the handlebars, revving the engine.

Conversation over. While I still have *no idea* where we're going.

The sun blazes as I secure the helmet over my head and lower the visor, instantly regretting my makeup. I'm going to be a sweaty mess by the time we stop, and while I know I'm hot, it's harder to make him regret his actions when I have mascara running down my face.

Laughing it off, I stride toward him and follow his move, lifting my leg over the seat, sliding on behind him. The vibrations make me giddy again, but when I lightly grip his waist, his body shakes and his powerful palms curl around my thighs as he forcefully yanks me into him. I gasp as my crotch slams into his back, and that gasp turns to a silent moan when he grabs my hands, wrapping them more tightly around him, locking them against his chest.

If my panties weren't wet before, they are now. Because... this man. *Jesus.*

Mason kicks off the stand, and the next thing I know, we're flying. Not literally, but my God, it feels that way. I've been on a motorcycle, but I was a kid and it was my next-door neighbor's paddock Honda. This is nothing like that.

It's like sin.

I'm not sure how much time passes as we cruise around in silence, the wind in my hair, my heart racing in excitement. I could spend hours like this, if my muscles weren't tense from clenching Mason's rock-hard abs and my ass wasn't vibrating so hard that it hurts.

We're in the middle of a residential street when Mason slows to a stop and lifts his visor, squeezing my thigh as he glances over his shoulder. "Can you jump off for a minute? I've got to grab something from under the seat."

My leg tingles when he releases me but I lift my visor, managing a "sure" before flipping my leg over the bike, groaning when the pain in my ass intensifies. "Is this where your job is?" I ask, shoving my hands in my pockets and leaning back on my heels, checking out the houses surrounding us.

Is he some kind of tradesman? A male stripper, maybe? *God, I'm funny.* If only he wasn't so touchy, I could ask him.

"Nope. But we're close." Mason takes off his helmet, drawing my attention away from those thoughts and I follow suit, removing my own.

"Are we walking?" I grimace, and laughter rumbles out of him. It's the second time I've heard him laugh, and I can't deny that I love the sound.

"You don't like being kept in the dark, do you?" His penetrating gaze bores into mine and I swallow my lust.

"That depends."

"On what?"

"On whether or not I trust someone."

Mason visibly winces but covers it with a quirk of his brow. "You don't trust me?"

"Definitely not. You haven't really given me reason to."

"I got you here safely."

"True. I'll give you credit for that. But I'd feel more comfortable if you told me what the job was."

He nods, a nervous expression washing over him that's so fleeting, it's possible I imagined it. "Okay. I can do that. Close your eyes. You're going to need something first."

"What?" I laugh incredulously. "Not a chance. Didn't we *just* establish I don't trust you?"

"We did, but now I'm asking you to try. Or you could wait here until I'm done." He shrugs and I curse under my breath.

"Fine." I huff and do as he asked, closing my eyes. "You better not be a criminal."

"Jenna. Jenna. Jenna. Are you stereotyping me because I own a Harley?" Mock disgust oozes from his words, and I poke out my tongue like a disobedient child.

"Hurry up," I gripe. That's not exactly where my mind, went but it's certainly less incriminating on my part.

Mason falls silent, leaving the only sound coming from my heart slamming in my chest. Tension courses through me, and I'm about to question him, when a shadow dances across my eyes, blocking the sunlight and making me quiver.

A warmth touches me and I jump, goose bumps coating my skin as Mason's velvety voice soothes me. "Hold still."

I freeze, my pulse spiking. I shouldn't be letting him near me, let alone standing here blindly, at his mercy. My heart continues to pound as the seconds tick over, and I'm ready to curse him when he gently tucks a strand of hair behind my ear, his fingers brushing my cheek. My breath hitches and I swear I hear him sucking in air.

"What are you doing?" I question, trying for an accusatory tone, but the words leave my lips in a whisper.

"I told you; I'm getting ready and I've got something for you." The air around me changes as he steps closer, and I can't handle the tension anymore. My eyes flash open, finding him dressed in a bright red jacket complete with a white faux-fur trim, and I stifle a snort.

"What in the world?"

Without so much as a smile, he steps back slightly and shows me a Santa hat, lifting it to my head. "You'll need this."

"Again, what? I'm not wearing that." I duck out of his way, shaking my head. "Not until you tell me what the hell is going on." I'm not usually a grinch. I've just reached my limit of shitty Christmases and I can't feel the magic anymore.

"Just put it on."

"No." I stand firm. "Not until—"

"*Please.*" The emotion in his voice makes me pause, and my lips part. "I know you're on strike from Christmas this year—it's been obvious since you arrived—but you love Christmas and I promise you're going to love this."

Something about the sincerity in his eyes has me nodding while my mind whirs. *When did I tell him I loved Christmas?*

Mason thanks me and steps forward again, a soft smile tugging at his lips while he positions the hat on my head.

106

"Perfect," he whispers, lifting my chin as he stares down at me and my breath catches. Mason's face contorts and he backs away, only stopping when I frantically reach for him.

God knows why.

His eyes dart to mine and I'm rendered speechless by the tenderness staring back at me. I hesitate, blinking a few times, snapping myself out of it.

"Sorry." I look away, my stomach churning uncomfortably. "Do I need anything else?" Mason's searching my face when I glance back, his bright blue eyes reaching into my thoughts, and I feel naked in front of him. Stripped bare and more vulnerable than I was when I was physically naked.

Why does it feel like he knows me? He can't know me. We just met. And yet...I've never felt more seen. Not necessarily because he can regurgitate specific details of my life, but because he genuinely listens. He takes notice. He acts like he cares.

Until he doesn't.

A vision of his harsh, passionless eyes works its way into my mind, and I involuntarily flinch. Last night didn't affect me. It was a meaningless kiss. Why the hell is my throat tightening right now?

Mason lifts his hand to my face again and I bow my head, dodging his intimate strike. "You've got three seconds to tell me what we're doing or I'm calling an Uber."

"It's a toy run," he rushes out, his genuine smile returning while my heart jolts.

"A what?"

"Every year the motorcycle clubs put on a toy run. Hundreds of bikers collect donated toys and drop them off at various trucks around the city. The toys are then given to disadvantaged children."

My skin tingles as everything I thought I knew about Mason completely washes away. "Who the fuck are you?"

"What?" A raspy chuckle escapes him.

"How did... Never mind." I shake my head in disbelief, a feeling of awe taking over me. This is one of those moments that's freaking me the hell out. I donate to a children's charity every goddamn year. If anything was going to sway me to get into the Christmas spirit, this is it.

But how the hell does he know that?

I'm still working through my shock when a moving truck pulls up beside us and Mason's friend Kai waves through the open window. "Are you ready, Jenna?"

What? My eyes bounce between Mason and Kai, my brows pinched. "Ahh—"

"Kai's going to take you in the truck," Mason fills me in. "I thought you might have more fun collecting the toys from the MCs as they ride past. Figured you'd get a kick out of watching tough bikers get emotional as they hand you a bag full of stuffed toys."

He winks and I snort to suppress a giggle. That's exactly the type of thing I'd get a kick out of. "It sounds perfect."

"Good." He grins and I hate that it's a little disarming, sending my pulse spiking out of control. I'm here for Jack. Mason said so himself. I'm on a mini vacation to catch up with a friend. Nothing more. Now is *not* the time for my heart to join the party. I've gone twenty-seven years without it. "Good," he repeats, squeezing my waist before he jogs to Kai's truck, opening my door.

I smile, swallowing the lump in my throat. Mason may be good, but I'm not certain I can say the same.

CHAPTER TWELVE
Jenna

After a quick hello and an official introduction, Mason disappears, leaving me alone with Kai. I wait approximately three point five seconds before I pounce, needing details.

"So." I spin to face him as soon as he starts driving, my brow raised in question. "This is strange, right?"

"What's strange about it?"

"For one, Mason doesn't strike me as the type to spend his day collecting toys for disadvantaged children, and two—"

"Wait." Kai cuts me off, a lazy smile playing on his lips. "That's *exactly* the type of guy Mase is. Nothing strange about it."

"Okay. Fair. I guess I don't know him. At all." A fire wells in my chest and I almost rub at the source. *Why the hell am I goddamn jealous?* I shouldn't know him. *We just met.*

"I don't think that's true." Kai interrupts my thoughts. "Some would say you know him more than most. At least intimately." He bounces his eyebrows, and it takes me a second to understand his meaning, making my jaw drop.

"He told you? I got the impression he was a private man."

"Oh, he is. I got him plastered. He spilled it all. Too much if I'm being honest."

"Jesus." I cringe. "Then I guess you heard how it ended?"

"Yep. And you'll be pleased to know, I told him he was a fucking idiot. Jack's a little shit. Mason's been taking care of him for far too long. It's time he put himself first."

Tension wraps around my heart. I *knew* Mason was looking after Jack, even when he refused to admit it. However, hearing it out loud hurts. "I agree that he needs to live a little, but it was just sex. Well, it would have been if Becca hadn't called."

"That's right. He mentioned that." Kai chuckles. "He said you stormed off when you saw the image on his screen." His lips curl and I shake my head.

"Put that smirk away; I'm not jealous." *Of that anyway.*

"Sure you're not. He told you she was a friend, right? She saved that picture to remind him he needs to get laid. By someone that isn't her. She claims he's happier when he does, and she's not entirely wrong."

I hide a smile because that's actually a little funny, but... "It doesn't matter."

Kai's eyes flash my way as his laughter ripples through the air. "You two are a whole new level of stubborn. The spark between you was visible from here."

"There's no spark," I scoff, but my creased brows give me away.

"Keep telling yourself that. You're here, aren't you?"

"I didn't get a choice."

Kai waves me off. "That's...not what I meant. As you said yourself, Mason's a private guy, and this event is something he holds close to his heart. It took years and a ton of physical threats before he finally let me be a part of it. Yet, here you are."

"What? Why?"

"He's going to punch me for saying this, but the gorgeous Harley that you undoubtedly frothed over is his dad's. His dad was a part of a motorcycle club—not the dangerous kind you see in the movies, but he was an enthusiast. He was always riding when the boys were kids. The toy run was his thing. And while Mase hasn't joined the club, he still continues the tradition. Jack's supposed to be here too. Though as I'm sure you've figured out, Jack is Jack. He lives by his own rules."

"Not a fan of Jack, huh?"

"Actually, I love him like a brother. Maybe that's why he's a pain in my ass."

"I can see it." I giggle and Kai's smile widens a notch. "I'm curious though...if Mason's likely to hurt you for telling me that, why say it?"

"Simple." We come to a stop behind a similar truck and Kai shrugs matter-of-factly, spinning to face me. "You deserve all the facts before you write him off."

"There's nothing to write off. I live in the US. He lives here. It was a casual hookup that never came to be."

"Like I said, keep telling yourself that."

"Okay, Mr. Matchmaker." I quirk my lips, fighting my smile. "Anything else you think I should know before the toys arrive?"

Kai's deep laughter once again fills the cabin of the truck until he pauses suddenly. "Yep." He winces. "Except I'm a dead man if I say it."

"Well, now I have to know."

"I like you." His smile returns. "Too bad you live in the US. You'd be good for him."

"Just tell me," I huff, blowing out a breath in mock frustration.

"He's a musician." He waves his hand, his expression neutral. As if to say "surprise." And... *Goddammit.* "Of course he is. Because what's better than a hot biker? A hot musician."

"I knew you liked him." He clicks his tongue.

"I don't *like* him. I think he's fuckable. There's a difference."

"If you say so."

Ignoring his jab, my curiosity sticks on his earlier statement. "Why will he kill you for saying that? Jack said he worked at a bar. Is he in a house band or something?"

"Nope. He hasn't picked up an instrument since his parents died."

"What? That's..." *Heartbreaking.*

"Fucked up?"

"Not exactly what I was going to say, but close enough. Why did—"

A thunderous roar interrupts my question, and I turn so fast the seat belt locks me against the seat. "Shit." I forgot I was wearing it. "Is it time?"

"It sure is. Come on." Kai reaches over and presses the release, letting my belt spring free. "You're not going to want to miss a thing. Mase will be part of the second group."

I jump out in record time, wincing when my ankle rolls a little on the landing.

Kai helps me into the bed of the truck as the first rider pulls up beside us, and my face splits into a grin. "Merry Christmas." The gruff biker smiles, handing me a red sack full to the brim. "Have a good day." His deep voice makes me giggle, and a joyous feeling takes over me.

Mason was right. This is going to be fun.

I 'm already surrounded with toys by the time Mason comes into view, and it's safe to say I'm having a blast. My jaw aches from constantly smiling, and it's been a long time since I've felt this giddy.

There've been at least a hundred motorcycle riders from various clubs passing by and we're only in the first hour. I'm in awe of how incredible this is. And well organized.

It's blowing my mind.

"How long does the run go for?" I ask Kai as Mason approaches. "How many trucks need to be filled?"

"It ranges each year, but at least another hour."

"It's inspiring."

"It sure is. Are you ready for your main man?"

I poke my tongue out and turn toward Mason. Rather than driving by, he pulls over behind us and lowers his bag to the ground, slowly dismounting off the bike. Even in his ridiculously corny Santa jacket, I'm still goddamn taken by him. Especially when he disarms me with that genuine smile of his.

Not that he realizes its power. He'd use it more often if he did.

"Jenna. Kai." Mason nods as he lifts himself into the truck bed, his smile softening when he sees all the toys. "*Jesus*. This is more than last year."

"Is it?"

"It is. I wonder if it's because of the stunning beauty manning the truck."

"Thank you, Mase." Kai pops his head between us. "That's nice of you to say."

Mason rolls his eyes, but they remain firmly locked on mine. "Are you having fun?"

"I am. Thank you for letting me come today." A jolt of warmth runs through me as my chest expands. I don't think I realized how much it meant to me until this very moment, staring into Mason's crystal-blue eyes.

Of course, he waves me off. "My pleasure. It was nothing."

"It was something to me," I admit, ignoring the tightness in my chest. "I'd lost sight of what Christmas was truly about. And you knew that, didn't you?"

He shrugs, once again playing it down. "I had an idea. I'm here if you want to talk about it. I mean, I'm sure you've already shared it with Jack, but—"

"You're an idiot, you know that?"

"The fuck?"

"You don't have to make everything about him. Not everything is."

An anguished expression flashes across his face, but he schools his features faster than I can question it. "You're right. I'm here if you want to talk about it."

"I don't. Not really. However, since you went out of your way to cheer me up, I guess I can throw you a bone."

"How very kind of you." Mason chortles, suppressing a full laugh.

"Shut up." I hide a smile behind my hand. "It's not a funny story." My eyes flash to Kai, but he's on the phone, distracted. He moves toward the edge of the truck, taking a bag from a beautiful older lady, admiring her tattoos as he jumps down to the street.

"That was well timed." Mason nods Kai's way and I smile conspiratorially.

"You'd think he'd planned it. To give us some alone time."

"Why would he do that?" Mason frowns and I can't help but laugh.

"I don't know. I'm not the one that got drunk and divulged all my secrets."

"Motherfucker." He cringes, his expression plagued with concern. "I was worried about that."

"What do you think you said?"

"I have ideas."

"Oh, yeah?" My eyes widen and I don't bother hiding my intrigue.

"Uh-uh." He bops my nose. "I believe we were talking about you."

That's right. *Dammit.* I blow out a breath, my nose scrunching. An outward representation of the knot forming in my stomach. "I don't hate Christmas. As you somehow guessed, I used to love it. It's just I haven't exactly had a lot to celebrate lately. If I was home this year, I'd have my friends, but...ah...my mom's an only child, and my grandparents passed away a few years back. My dad's family...well, they disowned him when he married my mom. I could have reached out to them after he died, but I'm kind of pissed off on his behalf. What the hell does it matter who your kid marries? Isn't it supposed to be about love?"

My voice rises and I pause, my eyes wide as I laugh softly. "Sorry about that. It's just..." I trail off when what I really want to say is *"you're really easy to talk to."* It's the way he looks at me, his soulful eyes boring into mine. The subtle nods in acknowledgment. The understanding. He listens with his entire body, and no one has ever done that for me besides Hayley and Blair.

"Anyway..." I lightly giggle, somewhat shyly when I am *not* a shy person. "My mom's always been a little...preoccupied with her own life. Even when Dad was around, she was always in her head. Though, at least I had him back then. Now, it's left to chance... Will she or won't she be around this year?"

"I'm guessing she's not?"

"Nope. This year she's in France with her new boyfriend. A guy she's known for less than a month. I'm not sure why this year was the last straw for me. But I lost a little of my light."

"I'm sorry, Jenna. I—"

"Don't be. I didn't tell you so you'd feel sorry for me. I'm fine. And that's not *fine* in the way people say it to make you feel bad. I'm more than fine. I'm *good*. Because of you."

"I didn't do anything special. Just invited you along for the ride. Literally." He smiles at his joke and I suppress a grin.

"Still, I'm grateful." *And I know you're lying. Me coming along is more special than you'd care to admit.*

"I can't help but notice that our family members have something in common." He raises an eyebrow and I laugh.

"Selfishness and a complete lack of responsibility?"

"You got it."

"Sucks to be us." My laughter increases, but it slaps me in the face, giving me a reality check. Other than telling Blair and Hayley about my mom before I left for Australia, I've never shared this part of myself. Not even to Jack.

"I don't know." Mason's eyes blaze as he stares into my soul, once again stripping me bare. "It doesn't suck to be me right now." The rasp of his voice makes me subtly quiver, and I swallow back my emotion.

"It shouldn't. This is incredible." I wave my hands around the truck, pretending I don't know he's not talking about the toy run. "How'd you get into this anyway?" I ask, changing the subject, putting him in the line of fire to shift away from my vulnerability.

Of course, he sees through my veiled attempt. "Come on." His lips curve in a mischievous smile. "You already know the answer to that."

"I do?"

His gaze locks on mine, sharp and assessing, pulling the answer right out of my mouth. "Okay, fine. Kai told me."

He nods, his expression turning serious. "What else did he tell you?"

"Nothing," I lie. I'd much rather hear him tell me about his life than have a half-answered conversation about it.

"Okay. Good."

"Why now?" I ask curiously, wondering if he brought me because he wanted to help or if there's more to it.

He frowns, and as if he's unable to hide anything from me, I see the moment he decides to be honest. "It felt right. With you."

"Why is that? And why do I feel it too?"

"I wish I knew. But—"

"Don't say it. Don't ruin the moment."

"What was I going to say?"

"That I'm Jack's?"

"Fuck, no. I was going to say I'm happy you came."

"Oh. Sorry. Guess I ruined the moment."

"Not possible."

Kai calls out as he throws a huge bag over the side of the truck, and Mason rushes forward, dodging bags, catching it before it hits the other presents. "Shit. Sorry." He cringes as he peers over the edge. "Kai's running out of space."

I follow his gaze to find Kai surrounded by bags, collecting them at his feet instead of interrupting our talk, and I smile in thanks.

He waves me off, reaching down and throwing us bag after bag, sending them spiraling in all directions, making us work while laughter fills the air. From both of us.

"What happens next?" I rush out, breathlessly, only pausing when we're finally done. "Please tell me you don't head home after this high?"

"We don't. Though I should warn you, if you thought this was Christmassy, the next part involves Santa and carols. With all the corny stuff that comes along with it."

"Right. Um. I don't know..." I trail off, jokingly, as excitement builds.

"You're coming," he states, his heated gaze unwavering

"Fine." I ignore my pounding heart, defiance in my eyes. "But I draw the line at sitting on Santa's lap."

"I know who Santa is." Mason's expression morphs into a confused scowl. "I wouldn't let you if you tried." He mumbles the last part to himself, and the jealousy in his tone sets my body on fire.

I like it. I like him. The problem is, I'm not sure I should.

In fact, I know I shouldn't.

CHAPTER THIRTEEN
Mason

Carols fill the air as one of my dad's best mates, Charlie, boasts about his daughter's achievements over the past year, specifically her engagement to a guy we went to school with.

I smile and nod at all the right moments, but it's impossible to give him my full attention. Not with Jenna's beautiful smile shining from across the lawn, her infectious laughter hooking me in. She's currently dancing to "Santa Claus Is Coming to Town," and her beaming happiness matches the children showing her the moves.

She's ten years old again, believing in the magic, and I wish I knew her back then. To experience more of this version of her, or any version where her eyes sparkle, her expression full of wild anticipation.

The longer I watch her, the harder it is to remember why her being here is a bad idea.

There's a reason I don't welcome anyone into this part of my world, and one of those reasons is standing in front of me. The other is God knows where, shirking his responsibilities, once again putting himself first.

"Mason." Charlie waves a hand in front of my face and I snap to attention. "Are you listening at all? Or are you busy planning your future with that gorgeous lass over there?"

"What?" I half laugh, half choke. "I'm listening. Jessica is engaged to Carl, and I missed my shot at marrying into your family."

"Well, well, well, who knew you could do two things at once?" He pats me on the back, his deep jovial laughter drawing a crowd, most of them shocked or uneasy.

Only, they've got it all wrong. While Charlie may look tough as nails with his long greying beard and sleeve tattoos, he's actually a softy when it comes to the people he cares about.

And since my dad died, I'm near the top of that list.

"So..." He edges closer, his demeanour morphing from his lighthearted nature to serious concern in less than a heartbeat. This is the part I loathe. I love Charlie like family, but he always manages to kill my mood, every time we speak. "Is Jack doing okay? You're still taking care of him, right?"

"Jack is fine. And yes, I'm still there. Whenever he needs me."

You'd think he was a fucking child with the way everyone treats him, including me. The sad truth is, he can't take care of himself. As much as I love my parents, wherever they are, I hope they realize they're to blame. If they hadn't spoiled him growing up, he'd be better equipped for this life. Although, I guess I have to take some of the responsibility. I've never asked him to grow the fuck up. I know I should. And lately, I'm so close to the breaking point, that it could be soon.

"You're a good kid, Mason. Better than most. Your parents would be proud." There it is. The reason I haven't sent Jack packing.

"Yeah, yeah. Thanks, Charlie. I try." I put on my best smile and hold out my hand to shake, feeling the weight of expectation in his firm grasp.

My phone buzzes, and he makes himself scarce, finally allowing me to breathe.

Until I read the message.

> **Jack: Have you seen Jenna? I just got home and she's gone**

Is he kidding me? It's almost three! He left her alone for most of the day and what...*now* he cares?

Spinning away from the crowd, I massage my temples and count to three, inhaling deeply.

"What's wrong?" Jenna's voice makes me startle as she grabs my arm, turning me to face her, concern etched in her features.

"Nothing," I lie. "Why?"

"You look like you want to kill someone."

Oh. *That.* I do. *I really fucking do.* "Would you believe this is my resting bitch face?" I smile with exaggerated force, and she erupts into giggles, until she seemingly realises where we are, frantically glancing around.

"Watch your language." She shushes me.

"My mistake. Has anyone ever told you you're a completely different person around kids?"

"Believe it or not, I figured that out for myself. What about you? Has anyone ever told you you're a marshmallow when—"

"They wouldn't dare." I mock anger and Jenna's face splits into a grin.

"You're not as grumpy as they say."

"And you're not as badass."

"Oh, yeah?" She steps forward, getting in my face. "Say that again. I dare you." The corner of her mouth tilts into the beginning of a smile, but she hides it away, and my chest aches for her.

I have never wanted to steal a kiss more than I do right now.

My heart hammers against my rib cage as an internal battle rages inside me. *Why should I hold back?* Why do I continue to put Jack first when he's never once offered me the same courtesy?

Oh, right, because I'm *"a good kid" and my "parents would be proud."* Charlie's hardened voice plays through my head, and *God-fucking-dammit.* I'm never going to escape it.

My phone buzzes again, but I don't bother checking my notifications before responding to Jack.

> **Mason: She's here. WHERE YOU SHOULD BE. We'll see you when we get home. If you're there**

He responds within seconds and my temperature rises.

> **Jack: Come home NOW. I want her back**

The fuck? I pocket my phone, my breath burning my throat as I secure a mask firmly in place, stifling my rage.

"*Hey.*" Jenna squeezes my bicep, her face marred with a frown. "Are you sure you're okay?"

"I'm good. Never better. Is it time for Santa?"

I fake a smile and Jenna attempts to smile back at me. Gone is her youthful happiness, and a wave of guilt takes over me. *Fuck.* I did that. I brought her here to get her out of her funk and I put her back in it.

"Jenna, I—"

"*Maasse.*" Kai cuts me off, stepping in front of us with a guitar in hand and a rebellious expression that has my stomach in knots.

"*Kai,*" I warn. "What are you—" The opening riff of "Jingle Bell Rock" answers my question and I narrow my eyes, my throat constricting as I struggle to take in air. *He wants me to play.*

"Kai?"

"I'm pushing your boundaries."

"Why here? Why now?"

"It's time." He shrugs like it's no big deal before his eyes flash to Jenna for the briefest of seconds, and my entire body tenses.

"You told her?" I accuse, my gaze bouncing between them, my simmering fury coming to a boil. "You were barely together an hour. What the fuck, Kai?"

"Mason..." Jenna grabs my arm but I shake her off.

"I can't do this now." Jesus Christ. *I can't do this ever.*

Pressure builds in my chest and I storm away, ignoring the waves as I pass my dad's crew, their faces blurry in my blind rage.

"Mason, wait!" Jenna's faint panic enters my mind, but I can't stop. If I don't get out of here, I'll never be able to breathe.

I'm vaguely aware of footsteps behind me, yet it's not until I reach my bike that I bother to slow down. Why the fuck do I do this to myself? And why is it worse now that Jenna's here?

After pulling my keys from my pocket, I pause and curse myself for leaving my helmet in the truck. I can't stay here. I'll ride slow, take the back streets and—

"What the hell are you doing?" Jenna grabs my shoulders, pulling me away from my bike, and the warmth of her hands soaks through my skin. "I get it. I do. But I can't let you go. I *won't.*"

The emotion of her voice works to calm me, but still, I shake my head. "You *don't* get it. You can't." My breathing picks up again and she steps closer, squeezing my arm almost painfully.

"Breathe for a second, Mase. Please. Forget what happened back there and breathe." My eyes focus and her expression sharpens, her flushed cheeks coming into view. I do as she asks, my eyes locked on hers, my heartbeat slowly returning to normal.

"Thank you," she whispers softly, her voice shaky. "I'm sorry about Kai. I didn't know he was going to do that. I should have told you he mentioned it."

"It's not your fault. He's not the only reason I had to get away."

"Am I the reason?"

"No." *Not exactly.* "I..." I trail off, unsure what I was going to admit, and her face drops.

Letting out a long sigh, I close my eyes, hiding from her sympathetic gaze. Only it lingers in my mind. I overreacted. My thoughts are so fucked right now, I can't see straight. I know she cares. I can feel it. "Kai wanted me to play," I admit, glancing back at her again, finding her dark eyes full of my pain. "I used to play at this event. Before my parents died. Kai mentioned he'd seen a change in me lately, and I guess he thought I was ready."

"But you're not?" Jenna's response comes as a question, but her fiery gaze tells me she knows the answer, and she's angry on my behalf.

"I don't know if I'll ever be ready. Though I can't blame him for trying."

"Why?"

"It doesn't matter."

"It matters to *me*." She steps closer, backing me into the alley behind us. "You think your thoughts are fucked up; you should spend a day in my head. We only just met and yet I feel like you know me. Isn't it only fair that I know you in return? I *want* to... I'll take anything you're willing to give me, but it needs to be *real*."

She's trying to make me feel good about myself, only it has the opposite effect, her words highlighting the asshole I truly am.

I *do* know her. Deeply. And I really fucking shouldn't.

Only I'm done doing the right thing. I always do the right *fucking* thing. If she wants *real*, I'll give it to her.

Spinning her around, I walk her backward until we're away from the road, the party we deserted no more than a distant rumble filtering through the air.

"I want you, Jenna." I cup her face, staring into her wide, wistful eyes. "Just this once, I want to be someone else, someone with passion, ambition, *life*. I want to be the one to fuck the girl who refuses to leave my mind."

Jenna blinks a few times before a blaze takes over and her hands curl into my tee, her knuckles white from the tightness of her grip. She feels the same. But I want to hear her say it. I need to hear her breath hitch as she whispers my name.

"I want you too, Mason. God only knows why. I want you to take me *now*."

Fuuuck. My skin prickles with need and I pause, considering how crazy that is for all of two seconds before checking for voyeurs and dropping to my knees. Pain shoots through me when I hit the concrete, and I welcome the sting, popping open the button on her jeans, lowering the zipper until her red lace panties come into view. "Christ, you're stunning." I peel the denim slowly down her legs, pausing when I reach her shoes.

Shit.

As desperate as I am to see her face when she comes apart, I'd much rather she enjoyed it. And this position isn't going to work.

Grabbing her hips, I spin her around and bend her chest toward the brickwork, my length pulsing when she automatically flattens her palms against the wall.

She rolls her hips, angling her pussy closer to my face, and I groan at the sight.

Taking my time, I glide my palms along her silky-smooth thighs, stopping when my thumbs reach her thong, massaging the skin beside her folds.

She bucks her hips, a soft hiss escaping her. "God, Mason. I really need you to touch me. Please."

"With pleasure." Though I'm not in too much of a rush. No one ever comes down here, but if they did, I'd hear them before they saw us, and the thought of that only adds to the fun.

I wait until she's shaking with need before moving her panties to the side and spreading her pussy, running my tongue through her heat. *Finally* tasting her. And... "*Fuck me*," I growl against her clit. "I knew you'd taste good, but this... You just became my new favourite meal." *Among other favourites.*

She mewls and I lick her again, swirling around her bud while the pad of my thumb lightly brushes her entrance. "Oh, God." She jolts backward, rubbing her pussy against my face, and a groan rips from my throat. Her arousal coats my mouth, and my cock twitches, begging for release.

As her breathing picks up, I nibble her clit and push a finger inside her. Her walls tighten and she shakes, straightening up, her body jolting when I refuse to release her, curling my finger instead.

"Oh, God. Yes." She melts into me before pulling away again, shaking her head.

"What are you doing?"

"I need you inside me, Mason. I want you to fuck me."

"Christ, Jenna."

Palming her ass cheeks, I give her a squeeze and nibble along the flesh, reminding her I have the power while preparing myself to do exactly as she asked.

After one last flick of her clit, I stand tall and rustle around in my wallet, grabbing a condom, lowering my jeans to settle below my ass.

Sheathing myself, I drag her backward again and pump my cock, lining up with her entrance.

Jenna sucks the tip of her thumb, glancing seductively over her shoulder, and I almost come in my hands. "I like when you get a little rough."

"Jesus, fuck."

I push into her, burying my cock before it's too late, grunting when she moans, "Yes, Mase. Fill me."

"Fuuuck." Curling my fingers through hers, I lift her hands above her head, crowding her in as I bite down on her shoulder, stifling my groans.

Her head falls back and she cries out, rocking against me, meeting my fervour as I pound into her.

"Fuck, you take me so good," I whisper into her hair and her body spasms, a high-pitched mewl escaping from her lips.

"More. Harder."

"Fuck, yes."

I jolt into her, pumping harder, my balls tight as my release builds. She cries out again, turning her head to face me, her expression full of the passion I feel. I capture her mouth in a messy kiss, but the moment our lips touch, a fire ignites in my chest and my heart clenches.

Her body quivers as I slow down my rhythm. Our tongues explore as I rock into her, my muscles tensing when she sucks me in, her pussy tightening around me.

She's close and I'm barely seconds behind her.

Releasing one hand, I curl it around to her pussy and roll her clit, grunting against her neck. "Yes, Mase. God, yes. Again."

I pump faster, my cock pulsing as I slam into her, rubbing her clit until she stifles a scream. Her orgasm hits and she bites down on her arm, her pussy constricting, pulling me over the edge.

"Fuuck, Jenna. Yes." My entire body tingles as my release consumes me, my movement slowing as we both struggle to catch our breath.

Grabbing her chin, I force her to face me and steal another kiss, sucking her lip into my mouth, groaning when a soft whimper escapes her.

I continue to kiss her, my lips gentle, letting her breath slow as she comes back down to earth.

The second I pull out, she twists in my arms, her eyes wide as she peers up at me. My heart jolts and... *Fuck. Fuck, fuck.* It's supposed to be sex, Mason. Just sex. We're in an alleyway, for fuck's sake.

Jenna giggles, bringing herself out of her trance, and me out of my head. "Well, that was a first." She pants, still a little breathless.

"What was? Sex in an alley?" I chuckle, hoping she doesn't notice the waver in my tone.

"Ahh. No." She cringes adorably. "I've never fucked anyone dressed as Santa before."

A short laugh bursts out of me and I relax a little. "It was a first for me too."

"Yeah?"

"Yep." I smile. *I've never fucked anyone I cared about.* Not that I tell her that. "I've never fucked an American," I say instead. And God, I want to do it again. Over and over.

"Good to know." She grins, fixing her panties before reaching for her jeans. "Now I think we have a party to get back to." My face drops and she rushes to reassure me. "No guitar and no questions."

I smile in thanks, as though she eased my mind. But the truth is, I'd do anything for her right now. And as scary as that is, I'm not sure I mind it.

"Is that really what you want?" I ask, just in case she's doing it all for me.

"It is." She smiles, seeing through my casual tone, understanding the deeper question. Getting me like I get her. "I'm good," she confirms, her voice confident. "And you owe the kids a dance."

CHAPTER FOURTEEN
Jenna

A strange peace settles in my chest as I watch Mason run around with the kids, his enchanting smile never once wavering.

We joked about being different people at this event, and this Mason is a complete stranger to me. There's a new lightness to him. An air of freedom. And it's obvious I'm not the only one that's noticed. Kai sees it too. I can tell by the many times we've locked eyes across the makeshift dance floor, his awed expression matching my own.

It could have something to do with what Kai told me about Becca's theory. That Mason's a lot happier when he takes care of his sexual frustration. Only this feels like something more. God only knows what it is.

A little girl takes his hand, dragging him farther away, and he summons me to follow, his eyes pleading as he curls his finger in a come-hither motion. I'd love to tease him. To pretend I don't understand. But with the new sparkle in his eyes, I can't deny him anything. More than that, I don't want to.

Which is not like me at all.

I'm a one and done kind of girl. Every once in a while, I might have a fling. Fool around with the same person for a week or two. In the past, one romp in an alley would not have me chasing after a man. Yet it only took one mind-blowing orgasm with Mason and I'm under his spell.

Because that's all this is. It has to be. Anything more than that is crazy. I'm sure Blair would have a mile-long list of cons for that pairing. The biggest one being that infatuation, lust, feelings... *love*... it's not enough. It's *never* enough.

Mason waves to get my attention, his mouth curled into a twisted get-me-out-of-here grin, now surrounded by at least four young tweens. I jog to catch up to him, pushing my thoughts out of my mind, laughing when his panic turns to relief.

"Thank you all for the dance, but my friend needs me." Mason points my way and I raise an eyebrow in question.

"Is she your girlfriend?" one of the girls asks, and I stifle a snort, hiding my smile.

"Not yet." Mason grins brightly, his stunning blue eyes flashing my way. "But you never know."

He avoids my gaze as the little girl swoons, and it would be the perfect moment to sass him. *If* I wasn't as smitten as she is.

Who the hell is this guy? And why does he hide him away?

"Now if you'll excuse me." Mason curls his fingers through mine and drags me away, waving over his shoulder until we blend with the crowd. Only stopping when we're away from the chaos.

"I can't tell if you broke their hearts or gave them reason to never settle for a lesser man. Either way, there were hearts in their eyes. You gave the first girl your complete attention for a good thirty minutes."

"What was I supposed to do when she kept asking for 'just one more song'?"

"A grumpy asshole would have walked away."

"Ahhh. In that case, I fucked up." He grimaces comically and I can't control my laughter. He brings it out of me.

"Mason, you can't pretend anymore. I've seen the real you."

"Have you?" His expression cools, trying to be that Mason again, but there's a flicker of doubt behind his eyes. "The truth is...you might be the only person I've ever been real with." His face scrunches and he shakes his head, as if purging his mind of unwanted thoughts, before smiling softly. "Anyway, do you want to get a drink?" He points to the bar across the street. "I'm dying in this thing." He flaps the collar of his Santa suit, adorably blowing out a breath.

"I don't blame you. It must be at least ninety degrees out here. Why are you still wearing it?"

"Sentimental reasons." He shrugs and I frown until he bounces his eyebrows and his meaning sinks in.

"I think Becca and I would be great friends. I understand her completely now. You just needed a good fff—"

"Shhh. Language." He shushes me like I shushed him earlier, and his happiness makes me giddy. It's infectious. Childlike. Magic.

If I needed proof that Christmas could be special again, it's standing in front of me. Mason and Jack lost both parents. My mom is still very much alive and I'm sulking because, for some messed-up reason, I placed all my magic in her.

"Hey, where did you go?" Mason lifts my chin, his magnetic gaze pleading with me to open up. To trust him. And I do. But I don't want to bring down his mood.

"I was trying to decide on a drink." I blink a few times, hoping it will snap me out of my Mason-filled daze.

"Gin and tonic?"

"What?"

"It's a drink."

"I know what it is. Why would you suggest that specifically?" It's my go-to when I'm out at a bar. But Mason doesn't know that. Jack does. "A gin and tonic would be great."

Mason's face lights up with a proud grin. "What a guess!" He cheers and once again, I can't help but laugh. "Come on. There's a high-top table out the front. I'll get the drinks."

As we cross the street, I take in the rustic-looking bar with its tea light candles and fresh flowers lining the tables and smile at how cute it is.

I sit down on the bar stool farthest away from the flowers, but thankfully, Mason moves them from our table to the empty one across the path and drops his coat in its place, squeezing my shoulder as he walks away. *You definitely can't put Santa's suit on the ground.*

He winks as he disappears inside and I smile after him. I'm sure he'd hate me for thinking this, but the playful side of him is more like Jack than he realizes. He just doesn't show it often enough, preferring to shield himself from the world, wearing his attitude as armor. Kind of like me.

Only my personality is a choice. A way to step out of the darkness my mom shadowed me in.

Mason's persona comes from his circumstances, from being forced to take on a responsibility he didn't sign up for. Getting nothing in return.

He's pushed everything aside to take care of Jack—his career, ambition, love—and Jack doesn't even notice.

My happiness fades as my heart aches for Mason. I wish I knew how to help. He's happy now, though something tells me it's fleeting. That like Cinderella, when the clock strikes midnight, reality kicks in and he's back to his old self.

Back to the man he doesn't want to be.

A flash of one of Jack's letters flits to my mind, and my stomach knots.

Gotta go. My brother's pissed off about something I did and if I don't talk to him about it, it'll become a whole big thing.
Sometimes I wish I was an only child.

Jack has no idea what Mason does for him, and I don't know whether to be angry or sad about it.

The warm breeze blows hair in my face as I stare off into the distance, and I'm lost in my head until a familiar face breaks through the mess.

Jack's staring at me from across the street, a soft smile playing at his lips, and you'd think I'd conjured him.

He waves when our eyes lock, and it's impossible to see him as the bad guy. Okay, not impossible, because no one could miss his careless nature and self-absorption. But he's a genuinely nice guy. He's sweet and caring and doesn't appear to have a hurtful bone in his body. Which is rare. I bet if he and Mason actually sat down and had an adult conversion, he'd be shocked to learn what he's put Mason through. I doubt he's ever taken the time to understand him.

I'd go as far as to guess that's one of the reasons Mason struggles so much. He needs a friend he can talk to, not a brother that takes him for granted.

I force a smile as Jack nears, and when he sits down next to Mason's coat, my nose involuntarily scrunches. Not that he notices.

"You're wearing a Santa hat." He bites back a smile. "It's cute. Here I was thinking you hated Christmas."

"What?" *Maybe he's more observant than we think.*

"I found the newspaper you destroyed this morning. The one with the giant Christmas tree on the cover. Unless that was Mason?"

"No, that was me. Your brother seems to love Christmas." I gesture toward the celebration across in the park and Jack subtly scoffs.

"That he does. Always the hero." There's a hint of sarcasm in his tone, but when I glance his way, he's smiling. "Did you help out with the toy run?"

"I did. It was amazing." A warmth swells inside me, and Mason's smile comes back to mind. "It's an incredible event. Have you been?"

"I sure have. It's been a while though. I don't think they do table service out here. Do you want a—"

"You made it?" Mason's dry questioning tone flits through the air, and Jack's eyes dart in that direction, his grin a little forced.

"I made it. I wanted to hang out with Jenna, and since you refused to bring her home, I thought I'd come to you."

I freeze, my eyes bouncing between them as my brows crease.

"She—"

"I wasn't ready to go back," I cut in, stopping Mason from having to justify his actions. "But now that you're here, we can all hang out, yeah?"

"Right," they both say in unison, tension sizzling as I awkwardly laugh.

"Jack, can I get you a drink?"

I stand up before he's answered and gesture toward the bar, needing an excuse to get away for a beat. They need a moment to sort their shit out, and God, I hope they do it while I'm gone.

After the initial awkwardness, Jack and Mason settled into their brotherly banter, while I sat back and listened, laughing at their jokes, questioning whenever they said something strange.

Who calls a sausage a snag?

And why the hell would I assume a "Servo" was a place to fuel your car?

Australians.

By the time we make it back to Mason and Jack's, with me getting a ride in Jack's car, they're buddies again. It makes me question everything I assumed.

"I'm sorry I've been MIA." Jack grabs my hand, stopping me from opening my door, his eyes locked on mine when I spin around to face him. "Tracey doesn't ask for help all that often. So when she does, I know it's important."

"You don't have to explain yourself. I've had fun."

"With Mason?"

"And Kai. You don't need to take care of me, Jack. I'm a big girl. I can look after myself."

"I know. But you came all this way to see me and I fucked up."

"No, you didn't. We're still good. I promise."

A beaming smile lights up his face, and I can't help comparing it to Mason's. When Jack smiles, a warmth coats my chest, but with Mason...I feel more alive than I've ever felt before. Like the curl of his lips has a direct line to my soul. It may be because he reserves his smiles for the moments that deserve them. But I think it's more than that. I think they're for me.

It's late when we finally get inside, and after saying good night, I head for the stairs, only stopping when Mason comes in from the garage.

"I'll see you in the morning?" I whisper so Jack can't hear me, biting my lip in an attempt to be coy. What I really want is for him to sneak into my bedroom and fuck me again.

Mason's eyes flare as if reading my mind, and he brushes past me on the way to the kitchen, squeezing my hand when Jack's out of view. "Or, I could see you sooner than that."

He raises an eyebrow and lightly slaps my ass, making me silently moan. But it's his beautiful smile that really does me in.

My heart jolts as the clock strikes midnight, and it's not Mason's reality that comes crashing down, it's mine. Because it's not sex that I want. It's *him*. I'd settle for his arms wrapped around me and his breath warming my skin. His comfort.

Fuck. I'm falling for someone that lives halfway around the world.

But that's not the most terrifying part...

I shouldn't be falling at all.

CHAPTER FIFTEEN
Mason

J enna's curled around me when I wake, her bronzed skin flush against mine, her hair tickling my cheek. I breathe her in, memorising her scent so I'll never forget this moment. Never forget that for a few wonderful hours, I was the guy I should have been. The guy who puts himself first.

And because of that, I'm here with Jenna.

After Jack crashed for the night, I waited for his snores before making my way over. Crept in on her like a stalker. Prepared to wake her if I had to.

Only I found her waiting for me. Perched on the end of the bed. Her eyes wide, her chest rising and falling with shallow breaths.

I'd never seen her more beautiful.

Jenna's bold and confident, yet in that moment, in her skimpy pyjamas, the strap of her silk camisole hanging off her shoulder, there was an innocence about her that had me cursing the world. Wishing I could spend the rest of my life protecting her from it. Despite knowing she's more than capable of doing it alone.

She stirs in her sleep, her naked legs tightening around me, and an image of our night comes back to mind.

Sex for me has always been a means to satiate a hunger. Forgettable. Sex with Jenna is otherworldly. The souvenir of kissing a path down her stomach is burned into my mind. The image of her muscles tightening as my lips brushed her skin may as well be tattooed on my chest. It's never going to leave me. I'll always remember the way she rode me, slowly, wrapped in my arms, her passionate cries playing on repeat in my head, like a note from my favourite song.

She'll forever be ingrained in my memory, and tomorrow she'll be gone.

Thank God, we've still got today.

Her soft breaths lull me back to sleep, and when I wake sometime later, the early morning sunlight peeks through the curtains, illuminating the dusting of freckles across her cheek.

I want to count them. To add to the list of things I know about her, because knowing it all will never be enough.

She stirs again, her face scrunching until I cover her eyes, and a contented sigh escapes from her lips. *I could stay here forever too, Jenna. If only you'd let me.*

I can't remember the last time I slept that well. Probably in the days before my parents died. When my only concern was whether or not my band got the sound check right.

And we always did. We were going places. Until...we weren't.

A door slams downstairs and I flinch, cursing Jack for reminding me of his existence.

While he had no reason to be pissed off at me yesterday, I could tell he was jealous, and I'm going to have to talk to him about it. I have no fucking idea what I'm going to say, or what any of this means, but I can't keep tiptoeing around.

Jenna's here for another twenty-four hours, and I'm not spending another minute pretending I'm happy for them to be bonding without me.

I don't want to waste a single second of our time.

Not when I'm refusing to acknowledge what her departure will mean.

"Ugh, why is it morning?" Jenna groans and I chuckle at how adorable she is. "Jesus, I'm sore. How many times did we have sex?"

"Four."

"Four!" She lifts her head to face me and my laughter grows.

"If you count the quickie in the alley."

"Oh, I definitely count that. I'm not going to forget it anytime soon. Who knew fucking Santa could be so magical?" Her eyes twinkle and my chest burns.

Every moment for her should be magic. She shouldn't ever have to question that.

"Uh-oh. What happened?" She bops my nose. "Are you pissed off at my disgusting talk of Father Christmas?"

"No." I snort. "I'm doing what I shouldn't be doing."

"Oh, yeah? What's that?"

"Thinking past tomorrow."

Jenna's eyes widen and she glances away, curling her face into my chest. She's quiet for a beat before jumping up so fast that it startles me. "Nope. We are not doing that. I'm getting in the shower and you're making me breakfast. Followed by a fun day at the beach. Okay?"

The fire in her eyes makes it impossible to say no, but I don't answer immediately. Not until she hits me with a Jenna special—a glare to end all glares. "Oh-kay?" she repeats as she stands in all her naked glory, her tone leaving no room for argument.

"Got it. Off you go then. See if you can wash away the bite marks on your ass."

Jenna's gaze shoots to mine, her throat bobbing as she bites her lip, trapping the flesh between her teeth.

And I can't let her walk away.

"Change of plans. We're spending the morning in bed." Jack be damned. We can talk later.

She lets out a squeal as I pull her back to the mattress, shutting her up with a kiss. "Are you ready for number five?" I cup between her legs, my fingers easily slipping inside her. "I need this pussy like my next breath." She pants with need as I flip onto my back, dragging her down on top of me. "I'm going to kiss this beautiful mouth while my fingers bring you to the edge, then I'm going to flip you over and wrap your legs around my neck, fucking you until you think of me every time you come." I curl my fingers while caressing her lips with mine, once, twice, three times before pulling away and whispering against her mouth... "Let's see how easy it is to ignore past tomorrow."

I catch the mirror in the hallway and laugh at the ridiculous grin that seems to have attached itself to my face. If Kai saw me right now, I'd never hear the end of it. I'm happy. And significantly relaxed. It's been a long time since I felt this good.

As if to remind me that I owe Jenna breakfast, my stomach growls at the same time the pipes grind, signalling that she's switched on the upstairs shower. Yet another thing I need to get checked.

This house may be grand, but it's close to thirty years old and it needs work.

I'm mentally adding to my long list of to-dos when I round the corner and find Jack blocking my way, the anger in his eyes making me jolt.

He's home. *Shit.*

"Did you have a nice fuck party up there?"

Jesus. I cringe, my chest tightening with a hint of regret. We should have been quieter. "I thought you went out."

"When? After I went to sleep? You were together all night. I saw you this morning. Curled in each other's arms. Since when do you have sleepovers?"

"You saw—" *Fuck.* That explains the door slamming. "Jack, you—"

"What the hell are you doing, Mason? You could fuck anyone, and you choose Jenna?"

"She's not anyone, Jack. I—"

"You what? You care? Is that it?"

"Of course I care. I wouldn't have slept with her if I didn't."

"Since when has that mattered? Don't bullshit me, Mase. Is this a way to get back at me? You've never liked anyone. You can't possibly expect me to believe it was any more than a quick fuck to piss me off."

"Are you kidding me? Not everything is about you. Why would I use Jenna for that?"

"Because she's *mine.*"

Jesus Christ. My stomach tenses with a mounting anger of my own. Now I know why Jenna was annoyed when I called her Jack's. It sounds fucked up coming from his mouth. But surely, like me, he said it in the heat of the moment.

"She's not anyone's property, Jack. Is that your way of saying that you want her?"

"It is. She came here for *me.*"

"And you left her alone. Come on. Be real here."

"I am being real. Jenna understood why I left. She gets it. She gets *me.*"

"That may be true, but do you know anything about her? Do *you* get *her*?"

"Of course I fucking do. We've been friends for *years*."

"You're right. I'm sorry." I raise my hands in mock defeat and Jack fucking smiles, once again displaying an inability to read a goddamn room. "I'm being sarcastic, asshole."

"Try me." He pats his chest and I shake my head.

"I'm not playing games. I care about Jenna. I—" His face drops, cutting off what I was going to say next. And thank God for that because I'm not sure what I was going to admit.

"I care about her too, Mase. I fucked up. I know that. But I can't lose her. If you hadn't stepped in, she might have wanted me back."

She might have wanted him back? Fuck. Tightness fills my chest until my ribs ache like they're close to cracking. "Don't buy her flowers," I blurt when he turns away, my heart pounding in my chest. "She's allergic to pollen and struggles to breathe if she sniffs it up close." I pause, my pulse racing, an anxious feeling coursing through my body. "She drinks vodka at parties but prefers gin and tonic, if you're planning on taking her out. And she hates wearing dresses. The only way you're getting her in one is if her acting role asks for it, and even then, she'll argue, questioning if it's really what her character would wear." Jack blinks slowly, momentarily stunned, and I don't blame him, because what the fuck am I doing? "She—"

"How do you know all of that? You only just met."

"How do you *not* know, Jack?" My voice rises. I knew he was careless, but I thought he was better than this. "How is it possible you seem to know nothing about her? It's been years as you said."

"Exactly, it's been years. I haven't seen her since I was nineteen and—"

"I'm talking about the *letters*. I've read them, remember? The same letters you read. It was all in there; you just had to pay attention—"

"Stop!" Jenna's broken voice cuts into my anger and I spin around so fast, I feel nauseous.

"Jenna, I—"

"You read my letters? All this time, I felt like you knew me. As if we had some kind of deep, meaningful connection, but it was all bullshit."

"It wasn't. It—"

"Stop," she repeats, raising a hand in front of her, turning to Jack. "And you. You let him read them? Is he the only one? Or did you share them around?"

"That's not—"

"It doesn't matter. This,"—she waves her hands around—"all of this was a mistake. I shouldn't have come. I thought I knew you, Jack. And I thought I was getting to know you, Mason. Obviously, I was wrong."

My body numbs as she rips my heart clear from my chest and storms out with it, undoubtedly throwing it in the bin on her way past. *Fuuuck. Why didn't I tell her?*

"Jenna—"

"Jenna, wait." Jack chases after her but I don't move, letting him have his moment.

I lied to her and she deserves better than that. She deserves a second to breathe.

Pausing when he catches her, Jenna turns to face him, her hands balled into fists.

"I'm sorry, I—"

"Wait." She cuts him off. "I may not have heard it all, but I heard enough. You don't want me, Jack." She reaches forward and squeezes his arm, her expression softening. "We're friends.

There's never been anything more between us. You're not going to lose me if I find someone else."

"You're forgiving me?" He frowns, confused. "Just like that."

"Not exactly." She smiles and the hurt behind the veil splits me in two. "I need some time. I'll give you the chance to explain, if you want that. But not right now. Right now, I need a moment to myself."

She's still talking to Jack, but her shattered expression lifts to mine, pinning me with her stare. I step forward but she subtly shakes her head.

"Please don't follow me. You owe me that much."

Without waiting for a response, she turns on her heel and rushes up the stairs, stealing my breath as she disappears out of sight.

Jack turns to face me again, and it takes everything in my power not to tell him to fuck off. Only this is on me. All of it.

And I need a moment myself.

"I'm going for a walk. Let Jenna be. Let her have the time she asked for. We can tell her everything when she comes back down."

I'm not letting her hate me until she knows how I feel. Until she knows exactly what she means to me. What she's *always* meant to me. Since I first read her letters.

Because that's what she deserves. Not time. I owe her an explanation.

I owe her the truth.

CHAPTER SIXTEEN
Jenna

My head spins as I slam the bedroom door, and my composure collapses. Along with my legs. I land with a thud and freeze, waiting for any signs that one of them followed me.

It's only when silence fills the air that I relax.

They listened.

Thank God, because...

Mason read my letters?

I had the strongest feeling he understood me on a deeper level, and now it makes sense.

It wasn't some soulmate bullshit like Blair would have had me believe, if I'd told her. No...he *cheated*. He snuck notes into the test. He *lied.*

Plain and simple, he lied. Even if it was by omission.

There I was, having flown halfway around the world like a fucking crazy person because of a stupid letter and— Oh, God. He *knew.* He knew exactly why I showed up at his front door. He taunted me with it.

While I laughed it off.

I have to get out of here. Australia. It's like I'm a different person in this country.

I'd never let anyone fool me back home. I'd never let myself fall...

I've got to go.

Haphazardly throwing my belongings into my bags, I listen for movement before rushing down the stairs, desperate to sneak away.

My heart races as I make it to the landing, the front door in my sights.

"Jenna?"

I startle, spinning around to see Jack standing in the hallway, his arms folded over his chest as he leans against the wall. "You're leaving?" He pouts, his puppy dog eyes making me pause.

"I can't stay here. You had to know that."

He nods, then steps forward, making me take a step back. "I'm sorry I never told you about Mason. That wasn't fair." The sincerity of his tone has my shoulders dropping in resolve until he keeps talking, almost making me laugh. "In my defence, I didn't know the two of you would become...ah...friends. I didn't think he was the type of guy that would ever take notice. Most people think he's an asshole that wouldn't stop to give you the time of day. I guess you caught him in a good mood."

I stare at him puzzled, trying to peer into his mind, to see how the cogs work. I don't get it. How can he miss what's standing in front of him?

"Do you really believe that?" I ask, my tone holding the incredulity I feel.

"Believe what?"

"That Mason doesn't take notice? That he wouldn't give you the time of day?"

"I said it, didn't I? Why would I lie?"

There's an innocence to his tone that makes my heart jolt, and for the first time, I wonder if there's more to Jack than I know. More than Mason knows. Because he can't be that blind. "I think the world of you, Jack. You've been the only constant in my life since college. And I don't want to lose you. Which is why I have to be honest. You need to wake the fuck up when it comes to your brother. You're wrong. He'd give you anything if you asked for it. And while I bet he'd never admit it out loud, he's been giving you everything since your parents died."

"Did he tell—"

"He never said a word. He didn't have to. I saw it myself. You say he's an asshole. But can you honestly say he's an asshole to you?"

"Yes!" he snaps but there's a question in his eyes.

"Okay." I laugh under my breath. "Just think about it. Please."

"Are you really leaving?"

"I am."

"Can I have your number this time?"

"Nope. You can write to me. I promise I'll respond. But maybe... keep it to yourself this time?"

Jack chuckles, but his expression tells me he's sorry before he says the words again. "I really am sorry."

"I know. Me too."

Me: I'm home

My phone buzzes across the kitchen counter as the various calls and messages come through from Hayley and Blair. Each one more panicked than the last. Other than a short "I'm okay" text, I don't respond. I can't. I wouldn't know what to say. I'm still trying to figure it out myself.

Not even the long flight and time to think helped make any sense of what happened.

How could I have been so fucking blind? I'm like my mom. All her boyfriends were wonderful until they weren't. Turns out, they'd been showing their true colors the entire time, and she hadn't fucking seen it.

The only saving grace for my sanity is that there's a difference between my mom's numerous men and Mason.

He cared.

He may have lied, or hidden the truth, but the devastation on his face when we locked eyes over Jack's shoulder is etched into my mind. He cared. Probably more than I did.

But it's too late.

I don't let my heart get involved. Ever. And this is the reason. It never works out. Not for my mom, and not for me.

My phone rings again, interrupting my thoughts, and I slam my eyes shut before peeking through my fingers, checking the screen. *Blair.* She's called at least twelve times since I first messaged a couple of hours earlier, and if I don't answer, she's likely to fly her ass over here.

"Hey, B." I keep my voice peppy, but there's no point. She knows it's a lie, made obvious by the loud sigh that plays in my ear.

"Jenna, thank God. You're back?"

"I am. I was getting in the way and—"

"Don't do that," she interrupts. "I want to be here for you, and I can't if you're lying."

"How do you know I'm lying?"

"Because getting in the way is your thing. You're Jenna Brooks. The star of the show. If anyone's getting in the way, it's them."

"Damn you for knowing me so well."

"It's a blessing and a curse. Sometimes I know too much." She giggles and the familiar sound chips away at some of my tension. I'm lucky to have her in my life and yet here I am, all *woe is me*. Acting as though my life is empty when I have two beautiful friends in her and Hayley.

"Thank you, B. You're a true friend."

"Uh-oh. It's worse than I thought."

"No." It's my turn to laugh. "I mean it. I don't think I tell you enough how amazing you are. I'm lucky you walked into my life that day."

"I think you walked into mine. And I'm lucky too. You gave me the kick I needed with Zane. Now I'm here to return the favor."

"It's a looong complicated story, but I promise I'm okay."

"I'm coming over."

"What?" I laugh again. "It's Christmas time and you're in Florida."

"It's not Christmas Eve until tomorrow, so technically it's not Christmas yet. Zane would understand."

"I'm sure he would, because he's obsessed with you. What about your family? No matter how I'm feeling, I'd never take you away from them. And I promise, I'm not that bad. I'm *fine*."

"Jen—"

"I'll meet you in San Francisco when you get home in a few days. I'll tell you everything then. Okay?" I hold my breath, hoping she'll accept my deal, and when she sighs, I relax.

"Are you sure?" she asks and while she's still worried, some of the concern has left her tone.

"I am."

"Okay. But I don't like it."

"I know. That's why I love you. Enjoy your Christmas. I'll call you tomorrow."

"Thank you. You better, or I'll be on your doorstep by nightfall."

"I don't doubt that. Bye, B."

I hang up and sink back into the couch, rubbing the heels of my palms into my eyes, a hollow laugh escaping.

Voices ring out in the hallway outside my apartment seconds before the distinct sound of Michael Bublé floats through the air, his smooth voice telling me "It's Beginning to Look a Lot like Christmas," rubbing it in.

It may look like Christmas, but other than my day with Mason, it hasn't felt like it this year. And as sad as that is, the worst part is that I miss him. It's been less than twenty hours and I miss him. Five days ago, we'd never met. Now there's an emptiness welling inside me, as though I left a part of myself in Australia. A part I never even knew existed.

My chest tightens as I imagine him and Jack waking up for Christmas morning tomorrow, and a fierce protectiveness takes over.

No matter how angry or upset I am with Mason, he deserves to be happy. He needs Jack to step up. Like he promised.

A knock at my door rips me from my thoughts and I groan under my breath. This better not be my neighbors goddamn caroling because I am not in the mood for that. "I'm sorry, I'm—" I pause, finding Mason on the threshold, his eyes red, his wispy hair mussed like he hasn't stopped running a hand through it since the moment I left.

"Mason?" My heart skips and I almost curse it out loud. *Stupid little muscle betraying my head.* I stand tall, my stare cold. "What are you doing here?"

Mason's eyes widen before his expression hardens and I see the asshole version I first met. "What do you think I'm doing? I'm here for a fight."

"A fight?" I rear back, shocked. "What the hell does that mean?"

"It means that I didn't take you for the type to run away, instead of calling someone out on their shit."

"Oh, right." I fold my arms over my chest, playing the part of someone that's not struggling to breathe at this very moment. "I forgot you know me so well." The venom in my tone hits, and I'm proud of myself for holding on to the fire when I thought it had left me.

Mason scoffs, but there's a slight waver in his voice. "I didn't get that from the letters, Jenna. I got that from *you*. It was obvious from the moment we met."

The fight leaves me and my stomach sinks. "That may be true, but what's the point? You live in Australia; I live here. We only had twenty-four hours left anyway, and that time is up."

"Actually, it's not. I have an hour left." He holds up his watch and I foolishly check it for myself, my heart jumping when I see that he's right. Though it shouldn't matter.

"It's too late, Mason." I stand firm while emotion threatens to clog my throat. "You're off the hook. I'm okay. It was a fun little vacay. Now, it's over."

I try to close the door before I shatter, but he slams his palm against the wood, his broken expression ripping my heart out of my chest. "I don't want to be let off the hook. I came here to apologise. To beg for forgiveness. Because I fucked up. I never meant to hurt you."

"Thank you. I appreciate the apology. But it's not necessary. It's—"

"Jenna, stop." His booming voice startles me and I rush to pull him inside, not wanting the neighbors to come out.

"Mason, what—"

"For one, I haven't actually said sorry yet, so your thanks are premature. And two, the fact that you're brushing this off only proves how much you're hurting."

"Oh, please." I sneer, ignoring the way my pulse races. "It was a few days and—"

"Don't do that. I may not know what I feel but I have never felt this strongly. And I know you feel the same. There was something between us, Jenna. There *is* something between us. You can hate me for what I did, but you can't deny that you also like me."

His words sting, but as true as they are, it's too late. "Whatever I felt... It's not enough. You had me at a disadvantage. I'm sorry you came all this way for nothing. You should go."

"You're not going to let me explain?"

"There's no need." *And I'm not sure my heart can take it.*

"That's not a no."

"Mason—"

"I first read your letters because Jack begged me to. He was going through a rough patch. Barely coping with day-to-day activities."

I frown, confused. "I wish I'd known he was hurting. But that doesn't make sense. Why would he need you to read them?"

Mason runs his hands down his face, blowing out a shaky breath. "Because he wanted me to respond. On his behalf."

"What?" I rear back as my entire body tenses. "You wrote to me?"

"I did."

"When? How many? Why?"

"I'm not sure how many exactly, but it happened more often than I'd care to admit and—"

"No." My chest heaves as nausea takes over me. "I don't want to hear it. Reading the letters was one thing but... I need you to leave."

"Jenna—"

"No. What the fuck, Mason?"

"I know. I'm sorry. But I'm also not."

"What? Get out." I shove him backward, moving around him to open the door. "I thought I wanted to hear you out but I don't. I'm sorry. But I'm also not." I gesture for him to leave, and he nods, accepting my decision way too easily.

Only, just when I think he's going to walk away, he pulls something from his pocket and holds it out in front of him.

"Take this, please." He doesn't give me a choice, grabbing my wrist and opening my fingers, placing the item on my palm. I glance down to find an envelope and flinch.

"Another fake letter from Jack?"

"No, Jenna." He sighs like I'm a brat, but I can see how much this is killing him. "This letter is all me. I'm not leaving LA anytime soon. Read it. *Please*. My number is at the bottom when you're ready to talk."

He squeezes my hand, walking away without a backward glance and my breath catches in my throat. I manage to hold myself together until the door clicks shut and I truly break out of my shock.

Mason's here. From Australia.

Some of the letters were *him*.

He flipped my world upside down. Now he's here. *Goddammit*.

Rushing forward, I throw open the door, my frantic gaze searching the hall. "Mason, wait!"

I can't let him go.

CHAPTER SEVENTEEN
Jenna

My heart hammers in my chest, each little pound an echo of Mason's footsteps coming toward me. He doesn't speak, but before I know it, he's standing in front of me, relief clear in his features, his soulful eyes locked on mine.

I want to scream, to tell him he broke my heart, but instead, all I do is blurt, "Where's your bag?" folding my arms over my chest.

I'm clearly all about what's important right now.

A flicker of surprise shadows Mason's expression and he bites back a smile, struggling to suppress it, undoubtedly seeing through my words. "It's downstairs with security."

"And what, they just let you in? Why would they do that?"

"My Aussie charm?" He shrugs and my eyes hurt from how hard I roll them.

"Get inside." Holding the door open, I gesture for him to walk through, turning his smile into shock.

"Really?"

"Yes, really. It means something that you're here. Fighting. It doesn't mean I forgive you. Not yet."

"I wouldn't expect anything less. I was prepared for you to put me through the wringer."

"Good. There's a couch through there." I point to the living room, ignoring the intense speed of my pulse. "Feel free to take a seat, or stand. Whatever. I'm going to read your letter in my bedroom."

"What if it doesn't change anything?" Mason raises an eyebrow, his confidence fading, giving me a moment of control.

"I'll text you to fuck off. It'll save you from my wrath."

"Thanks. I appreciate that." He chuckles lightly, his gorgeous smile trapping my gaze. The Aussie charm he mentioned must be working in full force right now, because my heart once again betrays me, skipping like a schoolgirl.

"I'll be back. *Maybe*."

"I'll be here."

I nod, turning to walk away until Mason calls out, making me wince.

"None of it's fake, Jenna. Not that letter in your hand, and not our time together this past week. It's all *real*. Remember that while you're trying to hate me."

My steps falter, but I don't look back, refusing to let him see how much he affects me. He lied to me. But he's here. He left Australia. Left Jack. He finally did something for himself and it was for *me*.

I hold my head high until I make it to my bed, collapsing in a heap the second my knees hit the mattress, tossing the letter out of reach.

Why am I struggling so much? This isn't me. I've never let anyone else dictate my feelings. Except my mom. And she earned that right after twenty-seven years of a relationship.

I've known Mason for four freaking days. Four.

But... No, no freaking buts.

Lifting my head, my eyes lock on Mason's handwriting on the letter and I physically wince. *How is it possible that I never noticed the difference?*

My mind whirs as I study the envelope, my fingers itching to stretch out and grab it while my heart holds me back.

What could he possibly say to fix this? He lied. He lives thousands of miles away. Nothing written in this little package will change any of that.

But I can't let it go.

Jumping up, I rip through the envelope as though I despise it and stare at the paper inside, my pulse picking up speed when I didn't think that was possible.

Taking a deep breath, I open the letter and immediately snort at the mistletoe drawing in the top corner.

As reluctant as I am to admit it, I needed to laugh at this moment, and I'll bet he freaking knew that.

Dear Jenna,

Thank fuck you're actually reading this.

Of all the letters I've written to you, this was by far the hardest.

The letters... the fucking letters. I'm sorry I never told you what I'd done. That wasn't fair. What I'm not sorry about is that I wrote to you in the first place. It's not something I'll ever regret.

In the beginning, it wasn't my choice, but it only took one letter for me to feel a connection to you. Actually no, it was one sentence and you sucked me right in. You'd written...

'Sometimes I wonder if anyone can truly survive this cruel world we live in. Then I think "fuck it," I'm going to give it all I've got.'

The truth is, I've been falling for you since the first letter I read almost seven years ago.

And now that I've met you, I'm not sure you see how amazing you are. Yes, you're confident and strong, but there's more to you that you seem to brush off or hide behind a veil.

Like the way you follow a compliment with something positive about the giver, never wanting to be the one to outshine them. You're unapologetic when it comes to your goals, yet apologise profusely if you forget a tiny detail about a friend, even if it's something you were never expected to remember.

You're loyal and caring while still seeing through people faster than most. And you're so goddamn driven that it awes me. You wanted to be an actress and you damn well did it. You followed your dreams, allowing me to live vicariously through your success.

Jenna, I wanted you before you showed up at my house, before you were famous... Hell, I wanted you before I'd seen your face.

There were times in my life when your letters were my vice, the only things keeping me positive in my otherwise fucked-up world.

I never wanted to hurt you, and I never set out to get you into bed. If anything, I tried hard to actively avoid that.

you deserve better than a man who lost his passion for life living on the other side of the world, but I couldn't let you go without telling you the truth.

I owe you that. And more.

I'd love to say I'd do it all differently if I had my time again, only that would be a lie. I loved every second of our time together. If given the chance, I'd happily spend that time over—fighting you, teasing you, fucking you in an alley...holding you while you slept. Anything to be close to you again.

To you we only just met, but for me, it's been building for years. I hope you understand me enough to see that I'm real. That from now on, I'll always be real with you.

This is me.

Take care,

Mason.

04xx xxx xxx

Take. Care. *Take care?*

Jesus. Jumping up, I rush over to my closet and grab Jack's letters, emptying the box onto the floor. Frantically opening each letter, it takes me all of five minutes to sort them into two piles—"take care" and "cheers." The letters are different. The tone is different.

My stomach knots.

Mason wrote ten letters. Ten! Including the last one. The letter that had me packing my bags and flying to meet him.

Jack. I went to meet Jack. Only it wasn't him.

Down to my very core, with every inch of my being, it felt like Mason knew me. Because he does. He's known me for years. And if he hadn't written that final letter, I never would have known him in return.

Tears prick my eyes and I throw the box across the room, my heart galloping in my chest. What do I say to that? How do I—

"Jenna." Mason clears his throat, and I frantically wipe my eyes, my gaze lifting to his. "I know you wanted me to stay put, but I heard a crash. Are you okay?"

"No." I shake my head, my voice catching. "I'm not even close to okay and I hate you for it."

"Jenna, I'm—"

I wave my hand, cutting him off, needing to get this off my chest. "I don't cry, Mason. Ever. Only you already know that." His gaze softens as he leans a shoulder against the doorframe, his piercing blue eyes holding me hostage until I blink. "*And* since you know me so well, I don't need to explain that I *never* do relationships. I don't do love. Not the all-consuming, can't-breathe-without-you love, not the love of your life, soulmate fairytale bullshit. Not even the boy meets girl, cutesy crush kind of stuff. I don't do it."

Mason nods but otherwise remains stoic, allowing me to continue, once again showing me that he gets it.

"You made me question things, Mason. You made me feel things I've never felt. In four goddamn days. Four days. Then you ripped my heart clear out of my chest. I don't do love because I don't want to feel like this. I don't want to be like my mom, chasing happiness from one guy to the next, always thinking the current one's her soulmate. Spoiler alert—he's not.

He never is. And you made me forget that for a moment. Until it all came crashing back on me."

"I should have told you the second I saw you, but I was pissed off. We'd... I'd been sending you letters for years, and you read one that's...let's face it, borderline pornographic, and you pack a bag to pay Jack a visit. Here I was falling for you and you fly thousands of miles for sex."

"You think that's what that was?"

"Wasn't it?" Mason's expression turns cold, while his eyes give away his hurt, along with the softness of his voice. "Why else would you wait until that letter? It's been years and you never once mentioned the idea of visiting Australia."

My heart jolts because he's right. I went because that letter felt like a hand reaching from the page and shoving me out the door. Like Jack was pushing me to go. Taunting me. Except it wasn't Jack at all. "Why'd you write it?"

"What?" He blinks as though my question confuses him.

"Why did you write it? What did you think would happen?" I hold his stare, needing to see every emotion as it flits across his face.

It seems like a million thoughts travel through his head before he settles on one, determination set in his gaze. "I think I wanted you to come."

"You think? But you still got mad at me."

"Because you did!" he yells exasperatedly, stalking toward me from across the room. "I wrote that letter. I wanted to do those things to you. But *you* were there for Jack. The guy that doesn't pay attention. The guy that asked his big brother to write to the girl he now claims to love."

"Why'd you do it in the first place?"

"Because I couldn't say no." His anger fades, and a heaviness settles in my chest at the sadness now plaguing his tone. "My parents were loving, supportive, incredible people. I used to think they were perfect. Looking back at it now, we were pretty spoiled. Jack more so than me, with him being so much younger. Neither of us were ever expected to do chores. We were never forced to do homework or activities we didn't want to do. They trusted us to make our own decisions and accepted whatever we chose to do." He pauses, huffing out a bitter laugh, and I can guess what's coming.

"That's where Jack's naivety comes from. Because while we were both good kids, it's not exactly the best way to raise responsible adults. They're lucky it didn't backfire on them."

I bite my tongue, holding back from pointing out that it did. With Jack anyway. Instead, I gesture for him to go on, offering him a soft smile.

He smiles back and his shoulders drop, a little of the tension leaving his body.

"The only thing my dad ever expected of me growing up was that I'd look after Jack. He drilled it into me over and over. 'Keep an eye on your baby brother, Mason. Make sure he doesn't eat any of his toys. You'll make sure Jack's doing okay at school, right? He needs to know his big brother has his back. We're out tonight; can you organise dinner for you and your brother? He won't eat properly if you don't.' Dad gave me every reason to resent having a brother, but I always did as they asked, no matter how much I hated it. If anything, a little part of me resented Dad for asking. And after they died, I would have given anything to hear his words again. 'I'm proud of you, son. We're lucky to have you.'"

My chest burns for all that he's been through, and I hate that I want to protect him. "He was an adult when they died. You shouldn't have had to take that on."

"He was barely nineteen. And a young nineteen-year-old. He'd never had to do anything for himself. I'm still surprised he survived four months in Los Angeles."

"I'm not sure he was alone in that either. He was part of a great team. His teammates all looked out for each other. His roommate too."

"And he had you."

I internally wince at how uncomfortable he looks, but he's right. "He did."

Mason nods a few times before shaking his head. "Anyway, I chose to take on that responsibility. I promised them both in the hospital before they died. Jack wasn't there. He had no say in the matter."

"I get all of that. I understand why you felt the need to help Jack, and I'm sorry you've held on to that pressure all these years. But that doesn't answer my question. Not entirely."

Mason sighs softly, his tired expression chipping away at my walls. "I first wrote to you because he begged me to. He made it seem like the most important thing in the world. And he was hurting. After that, I wrote back all the times I noticed he'd forgotten. When he'd been distracted by something else, ignoring all responsibilities. I knew from your letters that they meant something to you. I didn't want him to let you down. No, that's not true. I didn't want to let you down." His voice cracks as he grips the back of his neck, clearly uncomfortable with his admission. And I don't know how I feel. About him, about Jack.

"It wasn't Jack asking?"

"Not always, no."

Nausea coils in my stomach. This is so fucked up.

"What if I'd visited and fallen for Jack? The guy I thought was writing to me. The guy that didn't care as much as I was led to believe. What if his friend hadn't needed him? Or what if it had all played out the way it did and he asked you to walk away? What then?"

"If I'm being honest, I would have walked away. At—"

"I can't..." My eyes water because that's what I thought.

"You didn't let me finish. I would have walked away *at first*. Because that's what I've programmed myself to do. To protect him. Not anymore though. He *asked* me to walk away. And I did. But I walked away from *him*."

"What?"

"Why do you think I'm here? I've paid my dues. I've done all that I can, and I'm choosing you. No, I'm choosing *me*. For the first time in years. I'm choosing *us*."

As hard as I fight it, a soft smile tugs at my lips and Mason sighs in relief. "I'm happy for you. I am. But how would this work? You can't just pack up your bags and move to LA."

"You're right; I can't. It's way more complicated than that. But if you'll have me, I want to work it out. I want to start fresh and get to know you for real." He steps closer and tentatively cups my face, his gaze fixed on my eyes, waiting for me to react.

When I nod, a smile lights up his beautiful face.

"I'm not asking for forever. You're not ready for that. And while I'm well aware we don't always have time, I'd rather wait than risk never seeing you again. I'm here asking you for *now*. Begging you to give me a chance. Because I can't let you go. I can't let *us* go. I *don't want to*."

He whispers the last of his words, and my eyes widen as he unknowingly repairs a piece of my heart. Only I'm not sure I can risk breaking it again. Even if he's not asking me to. "What makes you think I want that anymore? You hurt me and I don't think—"

Mason grabs the letter from my hand and holds it above my head, interrupting my rant. I don't get the chance to ask what the hell he's doing, before he sinks a hand into my hair, his hold possessive, his lips taking mine.

A warmth runs through me as he pours everything into the kiss, coaxing for me to respond. And I give in, returning his kiss with reckless abandon, wordlessly admitting that he doesn't have to ask. He already has me, no matter how desperate I am to pretend otherwise.

He growls against my mouth, his tongue peeking out to trace my lips, and I melt into him, granting him entry, lifting to my toes to deepen the kiss.

Never wanting to let go.

I'm not sure how long we live in our moment of bliss before Mason pulls back, brushing a gentle kiss to my brow. Resting his forehead to mine, he leaves my entire body burning with desire and more emotion than I've ever let myself endure.

"I know you feel the same," he rasps, seeing into my mind. "It might not be as strong, but it's there. I can sense it. Give me a day, a month, a year. Anything to prove to you that I'm in this. To help you see that you want it too."

My thoughts run rampant with questions and fears, but they settle on something Blair said before I left, and I can't escape it.

"*You haven't settled down because you haven't found someone that sets your heart on fire. Someone you think about twenty-four seven. A guy or girl who knows everything about you because they pay attention, not because you told them. Because you're their entire world and they'd do anything to make you happy.*"

Mason *is* that someone. At least, he's trying to be.

"I'll give you until your visa runs out."

"Three months? I'll take it." He drops the letter and lifts me off my feet, spinning me around with a stupid grin on his face, and it tickles inside my chest. *God, don't tell me I'm going to end up all sappy like Hayley and Blair.*

"Put me down or I'll change my mind," I joke, but Mason's quick to toss me onto the bed, his brows raised in challenge as he kneels over me.

"I don't believe you. I think you've fallen for my charms. Next time I won't need the mistletoe to kiss you." I'm confused for a beat until a laugh bursts out of me, remembering the drawing on his letter. My smile cuts off when his molten gaze bores into mine, making me pause at the sincerity of his expression. "At least, I hope you've fallen for my charms, because God knows, I'm head over heels for yours."

CHAPTER EIGHTEEN
Mason

J enna blinks a few times, and my pulse races. I'm joking around, showing her I'm cool, calm, and collected. Only the truth is, I've been on edge since I got back from my walk yesterday. All because of the beautiful siren in front of me.

I'm enamoured by her. Taken. Under her spell. But more than that, I can't stand the idea of letting her go.

Because I never thought I would have her.

For years, I've been obsessing over a stranger on a page, all while existing for other people, playing my part, living the life I was asked to live. That shifted the second Jenna appeared on my doorstep, and when I realised she'd gone again, my life as I knew it blew up in smoke.

Staying behind was never an option.

I had to chase after her. We barely knew each other, but it felt like my world had gone dark and I'd do anything I could to bring back the light. The light currently staring up at me with doe eyes, her lips parted as she sucks in a breath, a very un-Jenna-like expression gracing her face.

I affect her.

Like nobody before me has managed to do.

And fuck, that's a good feeling.

"Dare I ask...are you speechless?" I bite back a smirk. "Because if you are, I'm kind of feeling good about myself and—"

"Shut up and kiss me again."

She doesn't give me a chance before a smile brightens her eyes, and she pulls me on top of her, pressing her lips to mine, her fingers curled into the material of my tee.

We're a mess of rushed undressing and wandering hands, as a desperate energy pulses through the air. But the second she's naked beneath me, her glorious body flushed with desire, I pause, savouring the moment, needing to take my time.

"Thank you for coming to Australia, Jenna. But more than that, thank you for being unapologetically you."

I've never been a missionary kind of guy. However, in this moment, I can see the appeal. There's something to be said about rocking into the woman you're falling for, her legs curled around your hips as she gasps your name, staring up at you with more emotion than you've ever allowed yourself to feel.

Doing exactly that, I sheath myself and wrap Jenna's legs around me, watching her in awe as I brush my cock lightly against her entrance, eliciting a soft mewl.

"I hope you're happy with slowing things down, because I have never wanted to fuck anyone the way I want to right now. But it's going to be different and it's going to involve feelings."

Her eyes widen before she schools her features, preparing to sass me, most likely trying to avoid the emotions threatening to overwhelm us both. "I'm not sure I—"

"It's happening. And you're going to love it." *I hope.*

Without waiting for a reply, I sink into her, lowering my body until she's moaning my name, filling her pussy as her walls suck me in.

"Fuuuck." I grit my teeth, suffering from the emotion overload Jenna was worried about. "I'm not sure I'll ever get used to how incredible you feel. How perfectly mine."

"God, Mase." Jenna bucks into me and it's only then that I start to move, my rhythm slow, purposeful, savouring as planned.

For a few heart-clenching moments, Jenna avoids my gaze, but when our eyes lock, everything she feels is staring back at me. It's raw and maybe a little uncertain, but the emotion is so deep and unrestrained that I know she's here with me. In the moment.

This is the real deal.

Pressing my lips to hers, I capture her warmth, kissing a path down her neck, my hand roaming from her hip to her chest, squeezing her breasts as I groan against her skin.

Her nipples firm under my touch and I rock into her, increasing my speed, thankful when she meets my fervour. She cries out, her chest heaving, her body lifting to meet mine, and as my heart pounds against her—for her—a thought hits me.

This is it. It has to be. Because I can't imagine ever feeling this way again.

Jenna whimpers, and I smile into her neck.

While she's not there yet—and her feelings may not be as deep—it's obvious she's close, and I'd wait a lifetime if I had to.

But I'm hopeful it's not that long.

I'm once again painted with a giddy smile on my face. I can't seem to shake it. I could be delirious from the lack of sleep since I have no idea what time it is in Australia right now, or what day for that matter. But I know it's not that. I'm lying in bed, Jenna's tucked under my arm, and I'm gliding my fingers over her naked skin.

What's not to be happy about?

"You're freaking me out," Jenna grumbles against my chest.

"Why?" I chuckle, refusing to let anything ruin my buzz.

"You're supposed to be my gruff, cranky Australian hunk of man, but you're giving me golden retriever vibes."

"Get used to it." I shrug, owning the change in personality. "I don't have anything to be *cranky* about."

"What about gruff? Can you stay gruff?"

Without a response, I flip Jenna onto her back and hover above her, lowering my voice to rasp in her ear. "I can be whoever you want me to be, Jenna. Only I refuse to pretend I'm not happy."

She swallows as I pull back, and I'm proud to note I've affected her again. "This is real. And it's happening. You and me. Some days I'll be grumpy, because that's who I am, but other days, I'll want to sing your praises from the rooftops. My happiness has taken a back seat for too long. I'm going to enjoy it."

Her face lights with a breathtaking smile, but she schools her features and fakes a frown. "Lucky I didn't say no. What would you have done? Turned around and gone home?"

"Hell, no. I had a plan B."

"Oh, yeah?" She sits up in all her naked glory, her curiosity piqued, and I marvel at the serenity gracing her features.

"Don't get too excited. I'm saving it for our first fight." I bop her on the nose, and she gasps, her brows pinched in mock annoyance.

"Are you already planning on fucking up? Does that mean something is coming?"

"No." My stomach sinks, my expression turning serious. Kneeling on the bed, I offer her my hand, waiting for her to take it before pulling her up next to me. "I'm not going to lie to you again, Jenna." My fingertips brush across her cheek as I tuck her hair behind her ear. "That I can promise you."

"Then why are you holding back?" She smirks, holding her stare until I relent, kissing her nose as I step off the bed.

"Fine. But I'll have to get my bag." I raise a brow in challenge, hoping she'll tell me it can wait. Only she doesn't budge, her stubborn nature willing to ride this out. "I guess I'll be back then."

Jenna watches quietly as I throw on my shorts and tee, calling out when I've reached her door. "Thank you." She giggles. "I like both versions of you. *Any and all* versions in fact."

"Good to hear." I chuckle without turning around, trying to ignore the way my heart reacts to her every word. "See you in a sec."

I'm only gone about five minutes and when I return, Jenna's half dressed in an oversized shirt and a lacy black G-string, making me *almost* forget what I'm doing.

Not that she'll let me.

With her arms folded over her chest, she raises a brow and smirks. "I'm waiting."

"And you're doing it beautifully."

Blood rushes in my ears as I riffle through my bag until my fingers brush over the hard case of my harmonica. Then, with as straight a face as I can muster, I spin to face Jenna again, holding out my hand like it's the most natural thing in the world.

Her eyes widen as they dart from my face to the instrument in my palm. "I thought you played guitar?"

"I do. And piano. And drums and..."

173

"Harmonica?"

"We'll see." I cringe subtly because I have no idea how this is going to go. I haven't played anything since my parents died. But I want to. For Jenna.

"We'll see?" she questions, rightfully so, because who the fuck tries to woo a girl with an instrument they've never played before?

"This was my grandfather's." I wave the harmonica around, huffing out a half laugh. "I never learned to play. But I taught myself two songs in the lounge while waiting for my flight."

"You taught yourself?" She gapes, studying my face for a beat, likely waiting for me to laugh. Only I'm not joking.

"I did. So...apologies if it sounds awful. I haven't actually played it out loud."

My chest tightens with uncertainty, and I chuckle to hide it, shaking my head. After a deep breath, I raise the harmonica to my mouth.

Glancing away, I blow a few times, testing the sound, wincing when it's too high or off-key, taking a few beats until I relax into it. Music used to be my life. I wanted to make waves. Travel the world. And I lost that for a while. Until now. I can do this. It's not going to be anything life-changing, but if it makes her smile, it's worth the pain.

Closing my eyes, the notes flow naturally for "Have Yourself a Merry Little Christmas," the bittersweet melody filling the room, the wistful sounds seeping into my bones.

My heart races as I pour my soul into the music, my brows drawn, my body so tense that I'm aching.

I don't move. I can't. It's been too long since I allowed music to fuel me, and it's impossible to stop.

Jenna's quiet as I play, but I feel her energy radiating around me, feel her eyes locked on my face, and it lights me up inside.

174

The final note permeates the air and I pause, catching Jenna's eyes on my lips, her awed smile making my chest tight.

"Wow. That was..." She trails off, her wavering voice matching the emotion in her eyes.

"A Christmas song?" I finish for her, though I'm certain that's not what she was going to say. "The plan was that I'd play it and you'd understand the deeper meaning."

"That I need to remember the magic of Christmas?" A smile softens her lips.

"No. That I'm here to bring the magic back. That you won't have to spend Christmas alone anymore. That you'll always have me. If that's what you want."

Jenna's smile drops and she sucks in a breath, a glint of wonder in her misty eyes. "I want that. It sounds perfect. What was the other song?" she asks, subtly wiping her eyes.

"Ah." A light chuckle escapes me as I scratch the back of my neck. "'Sweet Child O' Mine' by Guns N'—"

"Bullshit. There's no way you taught yourself that song."

"I never said I was good."

"You never said you weren't either. Are you some kind of musical genius?" Jenna appears awestruck but I shake it all off.

"Nah." I run a hand through my hair. "I was a songwriter, both music and lyrics, but I gave it up after my parents..." I trail off, glancing away, until Jenna forces me to look at her, much like I've done to her several times this week.

Her eyes bore into mine, sharing her strength, and a shallow breath escapes me. "My career would have taken me away from home, and my parents needed me there. Jack needed me there."

"And now?" She visibly swallows as if holding back something she wants to say.

"Now, I'm focused on you." I stare back at her, my expression determined, making her see my unwavering contentment. "Maybe I'll get back into it one day, but I didn't do this for me. I did it for you. To show you how much you mean to me. To show you a part of me I've kept hidden for years."

Her breath shakes before her lips pull into a slow, secret smile. "Okay." She nods, but I have a feeling she's not going to let me off the hook, especially after her eyes flash to the harmonica again. "I'll allow it. You can focus on me. For now."

And there it is. I chuckle to myself, ignoring the nerves that wash over me. I have no doubt that Jenna's going to challenge me. Daily. But for the first time in years, I'm ready for it. And I'm ready to challenge her right back.

"I think you're going to be good for me."

Jenna's smile widens, and she glances away thoughtfully before closing her eyes and laughing under her breath. "You know, I never really believed in soulmates or 'the one.' But I have to wonder if maybe there is someone for everyone."

"Oh, yeah?" My heart races as she turns back to face me.

"Yeah. And if that is true, it's possible you could be mine."

EPILOGUE
Mason

VALENTINE'S DAY

Jenna brushes a stray hair behind her ear and I study her features, my heart lodged in my throat, as her smiling eyes pass over the letter Jack sent.

I knew it was coming; he texted me to ask if it was okay. But this is the first Jenna's hearing about it, and while it's nice to see that the letter makes her happy, it's going to take some getting used to.

She laughs at something she reads then folds the paper and tucks it back into the envelope, her not-so-innocent gaze lifting to mine.

"Whatcha doin'?" she asks, struggling to suppress a mischievous grin.

"Waiting."

"For what?"

I stare at her deadpan, and her shoulder lifts in a half shrug before she tries to squeeze past me, miscalculating the distance she needs to stay out of my reach. I lean forward, easily catching her wrist. "Are you going to tell me what the letter says?"

"Which one?" She spins to face me, a coy smile in place as she straddles my legs. "I've been inundated. So many admirers." She bites her lip, and I can't stop my playful groan.

"Very funny. You know the one."

"This one?" She shakes out of my grasp and leaps onto the couch, holding the letter above her head.

"That'd be it." I stay where I am, despite the fact that it wouldn't take much to reach it.

Jenna's smile widens and I preemptively chuckle. "Oh, you know... Jack's professing his undying love for me. No big deal."

"*Jenna*," I warn and her expression softens. I trust her completely, and she knows that, but Jack's still a sore subject for me. Mainly out of guilt.

Things have been great between Jenna and me. We spent Christmas and New Year's together, getting to know each other. Now she's back at work, playing a spy in her first feature film, while I've spent the time she's on set exploring LA, taking in the sights of the city I plan to call home. I miss Australia and my friends. Hell, I even miss Jack being a constant pain in my ass, but it didn't take long for me to discover I belong here. Everything feels right. I don't have a job, a purpose, or friends—other than those Jenna has introduced me to—and yet I've never been happier. *And free.*

All those things will come. I truly feel like I'm finding myself again.

"What would you do if he *had* written that or something similar?" Jenna questions, bringing me back to the present, and the instant I picture that, I growl. I may miss him but...

"I'd be on the next flight to Sydney, ready to show him what's what."

Fire ignites in her previously playful gaze, and it almost distracts me. "God, I love a possessive man." She sighs blissfully and I stifle my reaction.

"I may have read that in a letter once." I shrug and Jenna snorts with laughter.

"I'm kidding. Of course, you can read Jack's letter, but Mason…" Her expression turns serious, seeing through my words. "He's okay, I promise. Kai's been keeping him in check." She raises an eyebrow and I can't stop the chuckle that bubbles out of me.

Kai offered to move in temporarily while I was gone. Actually, that's a lie. He offered to permanently move in on the proviso that he got approval to tell Jack what to do and turn the house into a bachelor pad.

I figured since he was doing me a favour, I'd agree to both.

It can't hurt Jack to have someone else pushing back on his childlike ways, and deep down, Kai's a caring soul. I'm confident he'll do the right thing, whether that means telling Jack to grow the fuck up or helping him out when he undoubtedly needs it.

"Did Jack mention Kai?" I ask, curiously. He hasn't mentioned him to me and it's making me wonder how they're really doing.

Yes, Jenna said I could read the letter, but I don't need to do that. I just want to know he's okay. Jack, I mean. Kai can look after himself.

Jenna smiles knowingly. "Jack will always be Jack. He doesn't usually discuss others unless he's pissed off at them. So, if there's nothing in here about Kai, that's a positive. He was chatting away like old times. You'd think Christmas never happened."

"What? Is he dense?"

"He's your brother."

"I know, but...why?" He basically told me he thought he was in love with her and now he's moved on?

"It's our holiday exchange. We started it as friends. And other than the times his annoying older brother responded on his behalf, it was never anything more than friendship." I stare at her unmoving and she laughs. "Him acting normal is a good thing. Yes, it may be slightly inappropriate to send a Valentine's poem to your brother's girlfriend, but—"

"There's a goddamn poem?"

"You're cute." Her eyes sparkle with mischief. "It's harmless. Nothing compared to the last letter I received. But as I was saying... I have a feeling Jack wrote to me because he's lonely. He's alone for the first time in his life, and you're halfway across the world. That can't be easy on him."

Shit. My stomach sinks as dread fills me. "Did he say that? He always called me selfish and now—"

"No, Mase. You are the least selfish person on the planet. You gave him eight years. If he didn't use that time to sort his shit out and learn to take care of himself, that's on him. I love him like a brother, but it's time he did it on his own. You have to make peace with it, even if it takes some getting used to."

"You're right. Thank you."

"If you're *that* worried, you could write to him every once in a while." She bites back a smile and I groan. No more letter writing for me.

"How about you tell him I said hi." I wink and a smile lights up her face. I'm not going to take away their letters. He can have that. I'm not heartless. I just don't need to be involved.

"Jack and I have a different way of communicating. It's this small device here." I wave my phone in front of her face. "It's called a cell phone."

"A what?" She fakes a gasp. "That would make life *much* easier. Can I have his number?"

"Not a chance," I growl, pocketing my phone, wrapping an arm around her waist, and pulling her roughly against me. "You want possessive. I'll give you possessive." I capture her lip between my teeth, gently tugging the luscious flesh as she melts against me.

"Jesus, Mase." She pulls back to stare up at me, her breathless voice making my cock twitch. "Jealousy looks good on you. Is this my Valentine's present?"

"What?" My jaw drops and I'm not ashamed to admit a panic runs through me. "I thought you said you weren't a Valentine's girl? They were your *exact* words. Are you trying to make me fail?"

"Fail what?"

"My ninety-day probation period. I've only got a month and a half left."

Jenna throws her head back as her rich laughter ripples through the air. "I think you're doing okay. I'd even consider upgrading you to permanent status. On one condition."

"Oh, yeah?" My heart jolts as I fight not to throw her over my shoulder, prematurely celebrating my win. "What's the condition?"

"You write me a song." *Dammit.* It was only a matter of time before she mentioned my music again. Two can play at that game.

"Deal, but... you'll have to face your feelings if I do, because the opening line is going to be 'Jenna Marie Brooks, I love you. With all my heart. And I'm never going to let you go.'"

Her breath hitches as I reach for her hand, holding it against my chest. She's silent for the longest beat, and for a minute, I think I broke her, until her lips curl into a smile. "I love you too,

Mason. But I have to say that's a pretty shitty opening lyric. You can do better than that."

I chuckle quietly as my heart fills with warmth. She loves me. It's official.

She's right though. I can do much better.

After all, I got the girl.

We may not know what the future brings, but whatever comes our way, we'll face it together because from here on out, we're living for us. And I've got to admit, it's my favourite way to be.

Thank you for reading Mason and Jenna's story. I had so much fun writing my first holiday romance. Here's to many more.

Curious about Hayley and Blair's stories? You can find their books as part of my San Francisco End Game series. Available now on Amazon.

BOOKS BY KATHERINE JAY

SAN FRANCISCO END GAME SERIES
Beautiful Storm (Luke and Amelia)
Delicate Storm (Easton and Paige)
Reckless Storm (Reed and Hayley)
Careless Storm (Zane and Blair)

SYMPHONY OF SOUND DUET
The Sound Of Silence (Jesse and Willow)
The Sound Of Forever (Jesse and Willow)

HEARTSTRINGS SERIES
When Nothing Else Matters (Summer and Dylan)
Still Here Without You (Joel and Delilah)
It Had To Be Us (Logan and Dani)
Truly Madly Deeply Mine (Wes and Lucy)
A Sky Full Of Stars (Thomas and Lainey)
Ain't No Sunshine (Nate and Cory) – novella

ALL KATHERINE'S BOOKS ARE AVAILABLE ON AMAZON AND
KINDLE UNLIMITED

Katherine lives in Australia with her hubby, two kids and a mind full of characters. She spends her days partaking in role play, building fortes and dancing. While her nights are spent reading and writing.

Katherine writes emotional and angsty romance with love that's worth fighting for and characters full of heart.

For more information, visit
https://www.katherinejayauthor.com

And if you want to stay up to date with all things Katherine Jay, come and join her Facebook Reader Group – The Angsty Lovers Playlist — for fun, exclusive content and sneak peeks. Or sign up to her newsletter via her website.

Are you following Katherine on social media? If not, you can find her on Instagram, Facebook and TikTok.

www.ingramcontent.com/pod-product-compliance
Lightning Source LLC
Chambersburg PA
CBHW051955220626
47052CB00004B/957